THE GIRL WHO
KNEW TOMORROW

Zoa Sherburne

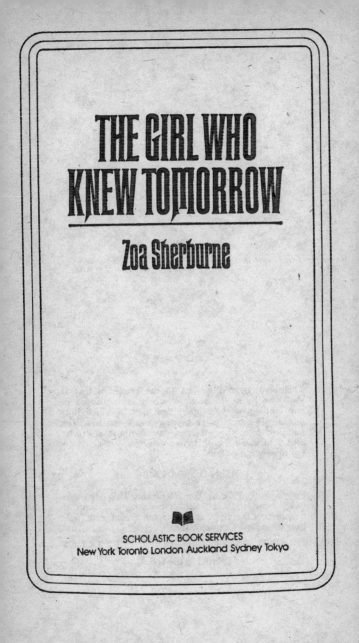

THE GIRL WHO KNEW TOMORROW

Zoa Sherburne

SCHOLASTIC BOOK SERVICES
New York Toronto London Auckland Sydney Tokyo

ISBN 0-590-09240-5

Copyright © 1970 by Zoa Sherburne. This edition is published by Scholastic Book Services, a division of Scholastic Magazines, Inc. by arrangement with William Morrow & Company, Inc.

15 14 13 12 11 10 9 8   1 2 3 4 5 6/8

Printed in the U.S.A.

01

ONE

Jeff called a little before eight o'clock. Angie had been dressed and waiting for over an hour. She couldn't help being nervous. Jeff was never late, and he knew she was supposed to be at the studio an hour before the show was scheduled to go on.

Her mother was pacing up and down, glancing out the window occasionally, twisting the wedding ring on her finger the way she always did when she was upset. "This is really *most* inconsiderate of Jeff," she said once in a tight little voice. "I've half a mind to take you down there myself."

"No one has to take me anywhere," Angie said mildly. "I'm a big girl now. I'll be fifteen in just a few days. If Jeff isn't here in ten minutes, I'll call the studio and tell them I'm on my way. Anything could have happened. He could be stuck in a traffic jam somewhere. Or something might have gone wrong with his car, and he couldn't get a cab. . . ." She didn't point out that Jeff wouldn't like her mother to take her to the studio. Jeff had discovered a long time ago that things went much more smoothly for Angie when her mother was kept in the background of her career.

She walked into the dining alcove where her grandmother was lining up some newspaper clippings on the tabletop, sitting still and straight in her chair. Poor Grandmother, she still wasn't at home in the New York City apartment, although they had lived in it for over a year. "Grandmother, what in the world are you doing?"

Angie's grandmother looked up, almost guiltily. "I found a bunch of these clippings when I was straightening some desk drawers. We really should put them in a scrapbook."

Angie picked up an old picture and stared at it without amusement. "Was I ever ugly," she said. "And my eyes look ready to pop out of my head. What was I so scared of, do you suppose?"

Her grandmother looked at her unsmilingly. "Of life, I imagine. Of having to stop being a child and becoming a person. In your case, a very famous person."

Angie wrinkled her nose and put the clipping back on the table. "I'm not all *that* famous," she pointed out, "and anyway I guess you don't worry about things like that when you're nine or ten years old."

The telephone rang and she flew to answer it, but her mother was there first. "Jeff? What on earth happened? We've been waiting and waiting. I was beginning to think. . ."

Her mother probably didn't realize how much she sounded like a nagging wife, Angie told herself, feeling a familiar stab of pity when her mother bit her lip and then wordlessly handed Angie the phone.

Jeff's voice was calm and unhurried. "I'm sorry, sugar, but we still have plenty of time. Could you meet me downstairs? I'll pull up at the entrance in exactly ten minutes, okay?"

"I'll be there," she said.

"What happened?" her mother demanded, almost before Angie had hung up the phone. "What made him so late? Jeff is always on time. He has plenty of other bad habits, heaven knows, but he's never late."

"He didn't say," Angie admitted. "He wants me to meet him downstairs." She whirled toward the mirror and brushed her hair back lightly, being careful not to disturb the heavy makeup. "I might as well go right away."

"I'll ride down in the elevator with you," her grandmother said, before her mother could speak. "I want to get some fresh air anyway."

Angie waited while her grandmother got a sweater, hoping that her mother wouldn't start putting two and two together. If Jeff was ten minutes away he was probably at Laura's apartment.

There were a half dozen teenage girls in the elevator. They were all dressed up for some gala occasion, a party or a prom probably. When the elevator doors swished open, they were chattering and giggling. As soon as Angie and her grandmother got on, however, the noise died away to a few scattered whispers.

"It is *too* her," one of the whispers came from directly behind Angie. "I saw her on television just last week, and my mother said that the doorman had told her. . ."

Angie smiled at her grandmother, who looked straight ahead and pretended she hadn't heard a thing.

When the doors opened into the foyer, the girls waited for Angie and her grandmother to leave before they spilled out of the elevator. From the corner of her eye Angie noticed some self-conscious-looking young men lounging against the wall. Most of them carried corsage boxes. They must be going to a prom.

The doorman smiled and stepped forward as Angie and her grandmother emerged from the building. Grandmother waved him away. They watched him find cabs for the young prom goers, and after the third cab had whirled away her grandmother turned and looked at Angie searchingly. "Those girls are just about your age. That's what you should be doing, going to dances and parties and having fun."

Angie grinned at her. "No, Grandmother. I should be going to the studio to be taped for a coast-to-coast television show. And I *am* having fun. It's a different kind of fun, I'll admit, but who would be willing to pay me a few thousand dollars to go to a prom?"

Jeff's car pulled up, and the doorman hurried to open the door for Angie, lifting his hand in a little salute as he did so. The doorman was impressed with Angie. His behavior was funny in a way, because he had helped hundreds of famous, really important people in and out of cars in his lifetime, and he was impressed with *her*. With Angie Scofield, not quite fifteen years old.

She smiled at him, waved to her grandmother, and slipped into the seat beside Laura.

Jeff pulled away from the curb and into the stream of crosstown traffic before he turned his head to look at Angie. "Sorry, sweetheart. Laura offered to broil me a steak, and we lost track of the time."

Angie shrugged. "It doesn't matter. I don't suppose they'll fire us. But Mother was getting nervous."

The mention of her mother was deliberate. Unless Jeff was an idiot he must know how her mother felt about him. And Laura Dennis was so young and pretty. If the school board only had found Angie a less attractive tutor. . .

"I'm sorry," Jeff said again. "I should have called."

Laura put her warm hand over Angie's. "It was really my fault."

Angie had the childish impulse to jerk her hand away. But the situation wasn't Laura's fault. If the distraction wasn't Laura, it probably would be someone else.

"You're being awfully quiet," Jeff said, when they were backstage at the studio and Laura had

11

been spirited away to the studio audience. "I hope you aren't mad at me for being late."

She looked at him soberly. "No, I'm not mad at you, Jeff."

They waited in the small green room for Angie's introduction. Jeff always waited with her. Sometimes they watched the monitor screen and sometimes they just talked, but tonight was different. They were uncomfortable together. Angie found herself wishing that she hadn't applied her own makeup at home. Jeff said that not having to go through the makeup routine was the mark of a professional, but tonight she would have been glad for something to do.

"I hear by the grapevine that you're going to have a birthday in a couple of days?" Jeff said in a determinedly cheerful tone. "Fifteen, hmm?" When she nodded, half-smiling, he went on. "Seems to me that such an advanced age calls for some sort of celebration. How about a party?"

She knew that the arrangements for a party already had been made, but she nodded again and tried to look really interested. "A party sounds wonderful, but they're a lot of trouble, I guess."

She couldn't think of anything more to say. A man stopped by and said hello to Jeff, and they talked for a moment. When he had gone away again the silence fell like a blanket.

"A penny for your thoughts," Jeff said, when the pause had become unbearable.

She put her head back against the sofa and smiled. "I was thinking of that other little girl," she said. "Grandmother showed me a picture tonight. It was a picture of me when I was nine or ten years old. Do you remember what I looked like then, Jeff?"

"You were beautiful," Jeff said promptly. "You had the biggest, scaredest brown eyes I ever saw."

Then the picture hadn't lied, Angie thought wistfully. She had been afraid. Even then she had been afraid. She kept her eyes on the monitor screen, but she wasn't really seeing the picture. She was seeing the other little girl, that long-ago Angie.

As far back as Angie could remember she had known that she was different. At first the difference hadn't bothered her too much. It was as easily explained as the fact that some little girls had curly blond hair and dimples and other little girls had straight hair and turned-up noses. It was as easy to understand as the simple truth that some people were wiser or stronger or more beautiful than others.

If her father had remained with them, her life might have worked out another way. Angie liked to believe that he had stayed as long as he could. She never talked about her father to the others, and once she had overheard her grandmother telling someone that Angie didn't even remember her father. Actually Angie remembered *everything* about her father. She could close her eyes and see him clearly, but she recalled a lot more than just the way he looked. His eyes were usually stormy, and he was always biting back words he didn't want to say. Tense and restless, he hated his job at the trucking company. He liked small helpless creatures, even mice, and Angie had never told

13

anyone that her father was responsible for her mother's failure to catch mice in the elaborate traps she set for them. Her father always found the traps and sprung them so that the mice could get away.

Her father didn't talk much except when he had been drinking, but he and Angie didn't need words. He hated the sentimental, explosive atmosphere in a house filled with emotional Irish women. His wife . . . his mother-in-law . . . his three daughters. If there had been a son, his life might have been easier. After little Stacy was born, however, her mother had declared that she would bring no more children into this dreadful war-ridden world, and her husband offered no arguments.

No arguments that Angie knew about anyway, although there were many times when she heard her mother weeping because her father had stayed away for the night, or had come home reeling drunk, or was running around with that dreadful Parker woman again.

Angie remembered the night he left them. She never told her mother or her grandmother, but she had wakened in the darkness to find him standing by her bed, his big hand lightly stroking her hair.

"I'm awake," she whispered and sat up, squinting through the darkness trying to see his face. Her sister Celia was asleep on the other side of the big bed, and not even an earthquake would disturb Celia. Across the room in her narrow bed her grandmother was snoring rhythmically. He put his finger to his lips and wordlessly she followed him out into the dim hallway.

"Why are you going away, Father?" she whispered. "Do you *have* to go?"

"Yes," he said, as if there could be no doubt. "I have to go." And then he shook his head. "How did you know I was going? What goes on behind those brown eyes of yours that know the answer before you have been given the question?"

"I just know," she said. "Sometimes I know about things a long time before they happen. Did you tell the others you're going away? Not just running around like Mama says, but really going away?"

She was nine years old. She didn't understand all the things that had occurred during those nine years, but Angie knew she would miss this weak giant of a man. He didn't tease her and call her pet names and then hug her the way her mother did. He never bought her unexpected gifts, and then complained about the cost and how children expected too much nowadays. Yet he looked at Angie with warmth in his gray eyes, and she could feel his love like a cloak that protected her through the storms of her mother's tempers. She wanted to cry because he was leaving, but she knew he would hate a scene.

"Will you write to us?" she whispered, and almost held her breath until he shook his head slowly. She was fiercely glad that he hadn't lied, because of course he wouldn't write.

"Good-bye, Angie. Don't let them beat you down. You stand on your own two feet and give 'em hell. You're the strong one. Will you remember?"

"Yes," she said. "I'll remember."

He reached out his big hand and brushed back a lock of hair that had fallen across her cheek. "You're like your grandmother, Angie," he said, and she had the feeling that what he was saying was terribly important. "Your grandmother didn't want your mother to marry me. She knew I'd never amount to anything, but when you came along she decided that maybe our marriage was worthwhile." He smiled, a sad smile that didn't make him look happy. "She loves you very much, Angie. She'll always want what's right for you. So you remember that, will you? If you ever have to make any tough decisions, she'll steer you in the right direction."

Angie nodded. She was sleepy, and she was beginning to get cold.

He didn't even kiss her good-bye. He just put his palm along her cheek and looked for a long moment. "Better hop back into bed now, before you catch cold."

She nodded and went back into her room, but she didn't cry. She thought about her father, following him with the eyes of her mind, down the creaky stairs and through the cluttered hallway with the ugly sideboard her father had always hated. She saw him walking briskly down the middle of the street, because her father was disdainful of sidewalks, and then waiting for the bus under the pale mushrooming bloom of a street light. Only . . . only he wouldn't get on the bus because a car would stop and give him a ride into New York. . . .

Angie remembered that she had closed her eyes and turned her head on the pillow, willing herself

16

to sleep. Tomorrow was a school day, and Sister Margaret would be cross if she had circles under her eyes.

In the morning, when she wakened, the memory of her father's departure was still fresh and clear in her mind, like something that had been written on a blackboard for her to read. She looked out the window while she waited for Celia and her grandmother to finish with the bathroom. Her father would be down at the waterfront now, looking for a berth on a ship.

Sometimes he used to take her with him when he visited the New York docks, although her mother said they were vile and smelly and not for the likes of a little girl. Her father loved to watch the big boats being loaded and then taking off for distant ports. He always had a sad, wistful look in his eyes when the whistles blew and the boats moved away clumsily from their moorings. He never once said that someday he would sail away on one of the big ships, that he'd visit strange lands and work like a slave and always have a secret regret that he had left her behind. He never said any of these things, but they were as clear to Angie as if he had shouted them.

"You are bone of my bone," he told her once when he had been drinking. "How do you like that? A little thing like you with all the mystery of the world in your dark eyes. You have your mother's black hair, and probably her temper, too, God help you, but you are bone of my bone."

He never talked to any of the others in the same way. Angie's mother said it was a crying shame the preference he showed among his children, but her father was perfectly honest about it. He didn't like Celia — she was a crybaby — and he wouldn't look at Stacy if he could avoid doing so.

Even when she was a baby the family had known there was something wrong with Stacy. She was too good and too quiet, and her eyes were a cloudy blue that didn't seem to focus very well. When she was a year old, Stacy didn't try to crawl or sit up by herself or reach for things. She was like a pale plump doll. Angie's mother fed her four or five times a day with the mistaken hope that eating would give Stacy the strength she needed to develop like other babies. Perhaps because she spent all her time with the baby, she loved Stacy more than all the rest of them put together.

The first weeks after Angie's father left home were difficult. Her grandmother was thin-lipped and quiet; her mother alternated between the belief that her father would return and that he was dead. That he would leave them without a word of good-bye, cutting the bonds cleanly and for all time, simply never occurred to her. He was her husband, the father of her children; the truth of the matter that for years he had not been her love or her companion did not dissolve these indisputable facts. People came and went from the welfare agencies. Angie's mother complained loudly about having to take charity. Her protests seemed strange to Angie, because at church they were taught that charity was something very special.

Finally the financial picture was straightened out. There wasn't enough money, but they could manage if Angie's mother cooked weekend meals at the parish house. Father Tracy was glad to have a cook, and he took care to overorder his food supplies so that there were always generous remains of roasts or turkeys or meat loaf for Angie's mother to bring home to her family.

But each time the postman came up the street, each time the telephone rang, Angie saw the hope that flared for a moment in her mother's eyes. The letter never arrived, of course; the telephone call was always from someone else.

"Don't wait for him to come back," Angie wanted to tell her. "Don't keep hoping that he'll walk up on the porch or pick up the telephone or sit down and write a letter. He won't. He's gone, and he'll never come back."

But she never said the words. Even at the age of nine she knew that a hope, however faint, was better than nothing.

One morning she wakened with the uncanny feeling that someone had spoken her name. Struggling up through the cobwebs of sleep, she rubbed her eyes and looked around the room in the early morning light. Her grandmother was snoring softly in her bed across the room, and beside her Celia was curled into a tight ball under the snarled bedcovers.

She sat up slowly, her heart pounding in her throat, and for a long time she sat motionless, her dark eyes not really seeing the shabby room with clothes piled haphazardly over the one chair and spilling to the floor. Neither was she really conscious of the dog barking down the block, or the hum of the furnace, or the sound of a faraway jet throbbing in the stillness.

Her grandmother wakened after a while, rolled over, and stared at Angie. "What in the world ails you, child? Get back under the blanket before you freeze," she said crossly.

Angie turned her head. Her grandmother's words seemed to release her from the spell that held her. "Stacy is dead," she said very softly. "She's dead, Grandmother."

Her grandmother's eyes widened fearfully, and then she shook her head, impatient with herself, annoyed at Angie. "Nonsense, you've had a nightmare. That's what's happened. Go back to sleep now. It's scarcely daybreak." She herself was half-asleep again; the last words were almost smothered in a prodigious yawn.

Angie slid obediently under the blanket. She was shivering, not with cold, but with an overwhelming sadness that her mother, who had lost so much in her lifetime, must now lose this child who was so dear to her. She still hadn't gone back to sleep when her mother's scream shattered the quiet of the house. Her mother slept with Stacy because of the undisputed fact that Stacy was delicate. She was inclined to colds, and if she kicked off her coverings during the night she didn't know enough to cover herself.

Her mother's scream went on for a long time, but Angie didn't move. She kept her eyes closed while her grandmother and Celia jumped out of bed and hurried to the next room. Almost at once her grandmother's cries matched her mother's, and Celia started to wail hysterically, but Angie continued to lie in bed, her hands closed into tight hurting fists thinking about Stacy, who would have been three years old in a few months.

At last sliding out of bed onto her knees, Angie put down her face against her folded hands and tried to think of a suitable prayer for the little sister who would never again sit on Angie's lap with her heavy head braced against Angie's shoulder and her cloudy blue eyes fixed intently on something the others could not see.

Mrs. Wilson, who lived in the two-family house across the street, came in after the funeral. She brought a cake on her very best cake plate, and she and Angie's mother wept together as if they shared a common loss. Just a week ago they had quarreled loudly about the Wilsons' dog being allowed to run free, and Mrs. Wilson had pointed out that her dog was less annoying than Stacy's incessant crying.

Angie would have liked to believe that from now on Mrs. Wilson and her mother would be fast friends, but things wouldn't work out that way. The Wilsons would move away in a few months, and another family would occupy their part of the house. Angie got up and made her way blindly out of the kitchen, past the adults who were still talking. She hurried up to her room and sat down on the edge of her bed, her hands clasped together and her throat hurting with unshed tears. Her grandmother had seen Angie's face as she brushed past the table. She followed and came into the bedroom, closing the door quietly behind her.

"What made you run off like that, Angie, right

in the middle of what Mrs. Wilson was saying about Dick's new assignment? It was very rude. . . ." She broke off as Angie swung anguished eyes toward her grandmother's stern face.

"Dicky Wilson isn't ever going to come home," she said. "He was killed . . . only . . . only they haven't heard about it yet."

"That is just your morbid imagination again," her grandmother said sternly, but Angie saw the fright in her eyes. "Don't you dare suggest such a thing, do you hear? It's sinful to pretend that you have some . . . some special communication with the Almighty. . . ." She broke off uncertainly as Angie started to weep, rocking back and forth on the edge of her bed, her thin arms hugged up against her chest.

"It's just that I *know*," she sobbed. "I don't want to know these things. I just do."

Her grandmother came closer, but she didn't touch Angie and her eyes were still frightened. "You mean you hear voices?"

"No. No one tells me. I just know."

Her grandmother came over then and put her hand under Angie's chin, lifting her tearstained face. "God help you, child, I believe you do." She made Angie lie down, and she brought a cool washcloth and wiped her face. "You lie here and try not to think about it. It's been a bad day for all of us. I'll tell your mother you're taking a little nap."

It was summer and so hot that the nights were breathless. Father Tracy came and talked to Angie's mother and grandmother about letting the girls go to a Catholic Youth Organization camp for a couple of weeks. Angie knew that the grown-ups felt her mother needed time to adjust to her loss. Perhaps Father Tracy thought that she would miss the two girls, which might help her to be thankful for the children who were still with her. There was nothing said about money, although one summer when Celia had wanted to go to camp her mother had dismissed the idea as ridiculous. Summer camps cost a lot of money; they weren't millionaires.

Father Tracy made all the arrangements, and although Angie's mother did some complaining about taking charity she didn't really oppose their going.

TWO

The camp was a nice one. Angie liked the counselors, and although she didn't immediately attach herself to a best friend the way Celia did, she got along well enough with the other girls in her cottage and didn't give anyone trouble.

Celia was in a cottage with the eleven- and twelve-year-olds while Angie was in the nine- and ten-year-old group. She quickly learned to make up her cot in the approved manner, to volunteer for unpopular tasks, and to keep all her things in perfect order. She was one of the "little ones," who were somehow special.

Every afternoon they had swimming lessons, under the guidance of one of the more energetic counselors. Angie loved the cold shock of the water and the clean feeling of the rocky beach beneath her bare toes. She listened to the instructor and tried as hard as she could, but she never became good at swimming. Celia hated swimming, but she played baseball and rode the mangy horses that were available, and her voice could be heard over any of the others when they had campfire sings.

Angie was glad she wasn't in Celia's cottage. It was good to be away from her for a while. She wrote to her mother and grandmother from camp, but the letters were stilted, simply stating that she was having a good time, that she missed them, and that she would be coming home soon. Although she could write fairly well, she still had trouble with spelling. She was ten that summer.

The two weeks at camp might have been without incident if one of the girls in Angie's cabin hadn't lost her ring. She was a spoiled whiney child named Deedee, and the ring was apparently a valuable one.

Miss Murdock, who was head of the camp, was quite upset about the disappearance of the ring. "Are you sure you had it, Deedee? We have a strict rule about valuable pieces of jewelry. It stated very clearly in the forms your parents were asked to sign that no expensive watches, rings, or cameras were to be brought along."

"But I always wear it. My gramma gave me that ring, and it has real sapphires in it," Deedee whined. "My mother will have a fit if I don't get it back."

Miss Murdock, who had been summoned to the

cottage by the distraught counselor, looked around at the circle of interested faces and spoke briskly but pleasantly. "Well, for heaven's sake," she said. "We don't want to stand around here and miss our swimming, do we? It's a very small ring, and it can't have gone far. Let's play a little game. We'll all march around the cottage, and then come in one at a time and go out the back way, and I'll bet that someone will find that ring on the floor or under a cot or somewhere . . . and put it here on the table! Shall we try?"

They went through the entire routine while the occupants of the other cottages stood around and watched, but the ring wasn't found.

"My mother will have a fit," Deedee sniveled. "My gramma gave me the ring, and it had real sapphires in it."

Miss Murdock was beginning to look harassed. The loss of a valuable piece of jewelry was certainly not going to look good on the records. "I've got another idea," she announced. "We'll all open our bags and look in there. A small ring could easily have rolled into a corner and been overlooked. . . ."

Angie spoke up clearly. "Deedee didn't lose her ring, Miss Murdock. She threw it away."

The circle of faces swung in Angie's direction. She was impaled to the spot by a shaft of curious glances.

Deedee's voice rose indignantly. "I did not either throw it away. It was my gramma's ring, and my mother'll have . . ." She stopped as Miss Murdock's hand pressed down on her shoulder.

"Well, Angie" — Miss Murdock gave her a bright

insincere smile — "what do you know about Dee-dee's ring?"

"She threw it away," Angie said slowly. "Only . . . she didn't know she was throwing it away. It was in the water . . . only the water was all cloudy and funny . . . like whipped cream . . . and her ring slipped off her finger and she threw it away."

Miss Snowden, who had listened silently, gave a little gasp. "This morning when you girls were washing up, remember, Deedee? Someone poured bubble bath into the washbasins, and you all were playing in the suds until I made you empty the water. Do you suppose . . ?" She never finished what she supposed, because half a dozen of the girls already were sprinting toward the place they had thrown out the wash water, and in a matter of minutes the ring was found. Deedee immediately slipped it on her plump finger, but Miss Murdock confiscated it.

"I'll take care of this until your parents arrive, Deedee. It was very wrong of you to wear anything so valuable to camp. I hope this has taught you a lesson." She looked at Angie then, and her eyes were frosty. "Do you mean you saw the ring when Deedee threw it away and didn't say anything?"

Angie shook her head. "No, I didn't see it. I just knew. I just knew it was there."

"She couldn't have seen it," Miss Snowden remembered suddenly. "Angie and Lorraine had washed up and were in the cabin making up their cots when the others started playing with the bubble bath."

"Then how did you. . ?" Miss Murdock started to ask, and then changed her mind. "Well, anyway we're all happy it turned out so well, aren't we? Now how about that swimming lesson?"

That evening Miss Murdock called Celia and Angie into her quarters while the other campers were enjoying a campfire sing. "I'm sorry to have to detain you two little sisters," she said with a smile that didn't quite reach her eyes, "but you can understand how important it is that we get to the bottom of this ring episode. I'll have to insist, Angie, that you tell me how you knew the ring was there. Did you put it there?"

Angie shook her head. "No, Miss Murdock. I never even saw Deedee's ring."

"She just knew it was there," Celia supplied helpfully. "Lot's of times she knows stuff. My grandmother says it's because she's black Irish and has second sight."

Miss Murdock's smile tightened. "Very interesting. And would Angie's second sight be able to help us locate the money that some of the counselors have been missing from their handbags ever since this session started?"

Celia looked at her sister and shrugged. "I don't know. Angie, do you know about the money?"

Angie sat down on the edge of a chair and folded her hands together. After a moment she spoke haltingly. "Only one of the counselors lost money out of her purse. The others just said they did, so you wouldn't think they were the one."

Miss Murdock stood perfectly still, and her eyes didn't flicker. "Angie," she said at last, "who did take the money?"

"A man," Angie said promptly. "A man in a dark red jacket. He came to repair a boat or something, and Miss Snowden's purse was sitting right there, so he opened it and took out the money."

"How do you know it was Miss Snowden? Did she tell you?"

"No," Angie said, "I didn't even know about the money until just now when you started talking about it." Her eyes filled with tears, and her voice was a little unsteady. "I just *know* . . ." she repeated.

Miss Murdock stepped to the door and called to one of the other counselors. "Anne, would you ask Miss Snowden to come here for a moment, please?"

Miss Snowden came, and she and Miss Murdock talked quietly for a moment before Miss Murdock turned and smiled and told the girls they could go back to the campfire.

Angie turned in the doorway and looked back at the two women, who were watching her curiously. "A long time ago," she told Miss Snowden, "you wore a big, *big* feather hat . . . and you danced. . . ."

Miss Snowden looked startled. "As a matter of fact, I did. How did you know?"

Angie shook her head. "I guess I just dreamed it. But it was a beautiful hat."

Some of the parents picked up their children, but Celia and Angie rode home on the bus, which didn't get in until nine o'clock at night. Their grandmother met them at the bus terminal. Angie's mother had a full-time job now, and they wouldn't see her until they got home.

"You look fine," Angie's grandmother told them. "Did you have a nice time?"

"It was fun," Celia said. "I won a medal for rowing and one for baseball and one for square dancing and one for . . ."

Angie's grandmother nodded approvingly. "And what did you win, Angie?"

"I didn't win anything," Angie admitted.

Their mother looked glad to see them. She had a new blue dress, and she'd had her hair cut short, but she was still Mother. She told them about her job on a small suburban newspaper. Angie could see that she was happy and excited about it. "Of course, it isn't a very important job, but it could lead to something really worthwhile. . . ."

Angie had the feeling that her mother wasn't speaking to her and Celia as much as to their grandmother, who was looking glum about something.

"You meet so many interesting people," Angie's mother went on. "Practically everyone is writing the great American novel. . . ." She laughed, and Angie smiled even though she didn't know what was supposed to be funny.

It was good to be back in familiar surroundings. That night Angie slept so hard that she had to be called two or three times in the morning, but her mother wasn't cross. She called Angie her little sleepy top and hugged her when she came in for breakfast.

After breakfast she sat at the table with them

and looked from one to the other. "Something very sad has happened," she said. "I don't want you to say anything about it, but on the other hand you should know. Dick Wilson has been reported missing in action, and his parents are very upset. We should remember Dick in our prayers. Okay?"

They both nodded solemnly.

Angie's grandmother never mentioned a word about Dick Wilson, not even after his parents were notified that his body had been recovered and was being sent home for burial.

Nothing was said about what had happened at camp either. Celia had the happy talent of forgetting anything that did not directly affect Celia, so although she talked a lot about swimming and diving meets and the baseball games, she never referred to the occasion when Angie had cleared up the matter of the missing ring.

Weeks later, on a Saturday just before school started, Miss Murdock visited them. She came right up to the door and rang the bell and asked to speak to Angie's mother.

Grandmother told her that Mrs. Scofield was not in. "I'm her mother. Can I help you?" she asked, and Angie knew by the tone of her voice that she suspected Miss Murdock of being some kind of salesperson.

As soon as she recognized Miss Murdock's voice, Angie came to the hall doorway. "Hello, Miss Murdock," she said politely, and then turned to her grandmother. "This is Miss Murdock from camp, Grandmother."

"I've been thinking about you, Angie," Miss

Murdock said. "I felt that I ought to talk to your parents and clear up the matter of Deedee's ring. I certainly don't want anyone to think that we suspected you, Angie."

Her grandmother's ears pricked up. She looked at Angie sharply and asked why she hadn't been told about a ring. What ring?

Miss Murdock spoke soothingly "Please, don't get the wrong idea, Mrs. Scofield."

"Cummings," Grandmother interrupted shortly. "My name is Mrs. Cummings. My daughter is Mrs. Scofield."

Angie's mother came home from shopping while Miss Murdock was still there, and the entire story was unfolded again. "It seemed so . . . so uncanny," Miss Murdock admitted, unbending over the cup of tea Angie's mother offered. "We were all so impressed, and I'll confess that I'm curious. Has this sort of thing happened before? I mean, we got the impression from things that Celia said. . ."

"No," Angie's grandmother spoke sternly, "of course, it hasn't happened before. It was just an accident." She pulled Angie down beside her on the davenport and patted her knee reassuringly.

Miss Murdock looked at her and then at Angie's mother. "I'm sure we are all aware that some people have this very special . . . gift. I think that Angie has it to a remarkable degree. There were two other things that happened in camp. One of the counselors used to be a dancer in a nightclub — oh, it was a very respectable nightclub, I'm sure — but Angie *knew*. She even described the costume, and she was able to identify the young man who had stolen some money from Miss Snowden's purse. Would you say that all this was accidental, Mrs. Scofield?"

Angie's mother didn't answer. She looked helplessly at Angie, who was sitting quietly beside her grandmother.

"Why did you come here, Miss Murdock?" Angie's grandmother asked.

Miss Murdock lifted her chin, quickly recognizing Grandmother as her adversary. "I happened to speak to a professor at the University about Angie. The man was very interested and would like to talk to her. They are doing some case histories on ESP, extrasensory perception. . . ."

"No," Grandmother said flatly. "Angie is just a little girl who is blessed with second sight. The Irish know about such things. You don't tamper with it."

Miss Murdock was beginning to be angry. "You're talking about superstition and black magic, and I'm talking about science. Angie is a very special child. You should be proud that she can contribute something to science."

"This month Angie will be going into the fifth grade. She has trouble with spelling, and she doesn't know her arithmetic very well. What good would she be to a university?"

"You just don't understand." Miss Murdock was willing to admit defeat. "Could I at least send Professor Taylor around to talk to you? Maybe he could make you listen."

"Run along and play, Angie," her grandmother said abruptly. "Say good afternoon to Miss Murdock."

Angie got to her feet swiftly, glad to escape. "G'by, Miss Murdock," she said.

"Don't go off the block," Angie's mother prompted automatically. "We'll be eating in a short while."

Miss Murdock took the hint and got to her feet. "I'm very sorry to have taken up your time," she was saying stiffly, as Angie let herself out the front door. She looked up and down the street, seeking a place to hide from Miss Murdock. Finally she decided that the cool empty space under the Wilsons' front porch was the best retreat, and she was safely entrenched there when Miss Murdock and Angie's mother came out of the house and stood talking for a moment.

She was too far away to hear what they were saying, but something about the friendly way they were looking at one another gave Angie a feeling of panic. She didn't want to go to the University, she wanted to go to the fifth grade. In the fifth grade she could start watercolors, and there were art classes twice a week. She wanted to sit in one of the front seats and watch Sister Nathan write on the blackboard. Next year she'd be in the sixth grade. She could try out for girls' choir.

She stayed under the Wilsons' porch until her mother called her for dinner, because, although Miss Murdock had said good-bye and driven away in her car, Angie was afraid she might come back. When she entered the house, she could tell that her mother and grandmother had been arguing about her. They stopped talking abruptly as she bounded into the room, and her mother kept looking at Angie anxiously as she ate her dinner.

That night, when her mother tucked her into bed, she took a long time fussing around the room. She didn't come up always to kiss them good night — sometimes she was too tired and sometimes she'd be watching a good show on TV — but this night she moved around the room, setting things straight on the dressing table, hanging away their clothes, chattering.

Angie was aware that her grandmother had come up the stairs, too, and was listening just outside the bedroom door. Grandmother didn't sleep in the room with her and Celia anymore. Since Stacy died, she shared the room with Angie's mother.

"Angie," her mother said at last, "did those things really happen at camp? Did you really tell them those things?"

"Yes." Angie spoke in a very small voice.

Abruptly Angie's mother sat down on the edge of the bed. Angie couldn't see her face very well, but she knew that her mother was excited about something. "Angie, do you ever know about these things because you *try* to know them? Or does it just happen . . . ?"

Angie frowned, trying to decide where this conversation was leading. "I don't think I try," she said slowly. "At camp I was anxious to go swimming and so were all the other kids, but Miss Murdock made us play those stupid games, so I told them about Deedee throwing out her ring. . . ."

"You mean, a voice told you?"

"No, not a voice." Angie scowled, trying to remember. "I saw a picture of Deedee throwing out the wash water with all the foamy stuff in it . . . and the ring was there . . . and there were trees all over the place so I knew it had to be at camp."

Angie's grandmother came quietly into the room and stood at the foot of the bed.

"That's right," Celia volunteered from her side of the bed. "It happened just like that, but a lot of the kids thought Angie took that ring and put it there."

"Hush, Celia," their mother said so gently that Angie knew she was deep in some complicated train of thought. Normally her mother would have yelled at Celia to shut up.

"The children are tired," Angie's grandmother said. "Come along, Jessie. We can talk about this later."

Her mother started to say something, then changed her mind and got up from the bed and went out of the room. Grandmother stood there for another moment before she kissed Angie's cheek. "Pay it no mind, Angela," she whispered. "Just sleep now, and we'll all pretend it never happened."

She didn't kiss Celia good night. She just clicked off the hall light and went noiselessly down the stairs. Usually Grandmother didn't kiss the children unless they were going on a trip or coming home again or there was a special occasion like a birthday.

In the darkness Celia spoke crossly. "If you can tell all these things for other people, how come you can't tell us about Father? Where he is and when's he coming home."

Angie chose her words carefully. "I don't know.

It's just that sometimes I know and sometimes I don't know."

Celia raised herself on one elbow and peered suspiciously through the darkness. "I think you know all right. You just don't want to tell. Come on, Angie, you can tell me. I won't tell the others. Is he in jail or dead or what?"

"Shut up!" Angie yelled suddenly. "Just shut up or I'll tell Mother about what you did last year when you played hookey and you told Sister Nathan you were sick and going home."

There was a thudding silence in the bedroom, and then Angie's mother's voice floated up the stairs. "Girls, quiet down or I'll come up there and attend to you."

THREE

Angie loved the fifth grade. She had a lay teacher named Miss Pilgrim, who was young and pretty, and she made friends with her classmates, although Angie had never been very good about making friends.

The nuns were good to her and Celia; they were always especially kind to the children who came from broken homes.

"Do we have a broken home?" she asked her grandmother one afternoon, when she came in from school. "Does a broken home mean there are cracks in the ceiling and the porch steps are crooked?"

"No, you can have a broken home even when you live in a big mansion," her grandmother told her. "That's one thing about money, Angie. It can't buy happiness. Why, I remember . . ." and she went off into a long story about her cousin that Angie had heard a dozen times.

She waited, her foot hooked over the rung of her chair, until the story was finished, and then she asked her question again. "But do we have a broken home?"

Her grandmother looked at her sadly. "I expect you could say so. A broken home generally means that one of the parents is missing — either divorced or just run off, like your father." And then, being grandmother, she asked sharply, "Why? Who was talking about this being a broken home?"

"Miss Pilgrim," Angie said promptly. "Only she wasn't talking about this house. But once she looked at me while she was telling us . . ." she broke off, trying to remember, but her grandmother interrupted swiftly.

"Never mind. Anyway, broken home or no, we have a good life, and I hope you don't forget it."

They did have a good life. In a strange way they had a better life than when Angie's father was with them. There wasn't so much quarreling, and, of course, Stacy was no longer there to absorb all of her mother's love and attention. They had good nourishing meals, thanks to Grandmother's cooking, both girls had warm winter coats, and Angie's mother got a real bargain in a used car, which she needed for doing errands in their suburban town.

Miss Murdock came back once again when Angie was at school and her mother was working, but Grandmother sent her away. She told them about the visit at dinner. "That Murdock woman was here again," she said. "She left word for you to call her, Jessie, but I told her you probably wouldn't have time." Just the way she spoke Angie knew that her grandmother was braced for an argument.

But Angie's mother went on eating. "You did the right thing," she said. "After all, Angie is just a little girl and why should some university professor get all the credit for her talent? I've been reading up on this sort of thing. It isn't just a gift, it's a special talent Angie has. Only you can't push it, not until she's more mature."

"What do you mean, push it?" Grandmother asked sharply.

Angie's mother shrugged. "Nothing, really. Except that I've been thinking. We know that Angie has this special something, and it stands to reason that she has it for some purpose. She could help people. She could find things that were lost; she's already proven that. She probably could help the police solve crimes. . . ."

Angie pushed back her chair. "No," she said. "No, I couldn't."

Her mother reached out and pulled Angie close to her. "Honey, don't worry about it. No one is going to force you to do anything. But I want you to promise me something. Whenever you, whenever this thing happens, whenever you know something, I want you to come and tell me. Will you do that?"

"Why?" Angie asked. She wasn't so frightened now that her mother's arm was around her and her mother was smiling. But still . . . "Why?" she asked again.

"So that she can write it down in her stupid journal, that's why," Angie's grandmother said explosively. "So that she can keep a record for that university professor."

Angie's mother looked up, her eyes flashing. "It's none of your business, Mother. I wish you'd keep out of this."

"Well, I won't," Grandmother said flatly. "You think I don't know what you have in mind, Jessie? Exploiting this child as if she were some sort of freak, putting her on the stage, like as not. . ."

"I have no intention of doing anything that isn't best for Angie," her mother said firmly. "Angie is just a child, but I'm not. I can look ahead and see that this . . . this gift of hers might provide all the security she needs. I've been talking to people, and they are all interested and excited about Angie. There is a man. . . ."

"I'll bet there is," Grandmother interrupted with a sniff.

Angie's mother tightened her arm around Angie's shoulders. "Mother, sometimes you have a one-track mind," she said softly. "Angie has a rare gift. . . ."

Angie shook free of her mother's encircling arm. "It doesn't matter," she said. "Because I don't see things anymore. I don't know about things before they happen."

"You do too." Celia abandoned her meat and potatoes and spoke up for the first time. "Just this week that boy in your room came to school almost crying because his dog hadn't come home and he was afraid it got hit by a car. You told him it was locked up somewhere in a dark place with a little bitty window with a broken shade, and he remembered seeing a shed like that on the next block, and he went and found the dog." She looked at her mother triumphantly. "She really did. Miss Pilgrim told the nuns and teachers, and then somebody told them about that stuff at camp, and now the kids think Angie's some kind of a nut. . . ."

"*You* told them," Angie said. "You told them about what really happened, and then you told them a lot of lies, too."

"I did not." Celia flushed angrily. "Anyway Miss Pilgrim made me tell her that stuff."

"No, she didn't. You didn't even tell Miss Pilgrim. You told Sister Elizabeth Mary, and she said you weren't to repeat things that couldn't possibly be true."

Grandmother got up from the table and took Angie by the hand. "We won't talk about it anymore. Angie, will you run down to Miss Perkins and get me those old coats she's been saving for my braided rugs before it gets dark?"

Angie looked up into the tired face gratefully. "Yes, I'll go," she said, happy to make her escape from what promised to be another quarrel between her mother and her grandmother.

Skipping down the road toward the Perkins' house she found herself thinking how pleasant it would be if she lived with just her grandmother. Not that she didn't love her mother, but in some vague way she was afraid of her mother. She felt as though her mother were pushing her toward some shadowy world that frightened her.

When she met Jeff Granger she knew why she had been afraid.

Her mother had talked a lot about some man at work who kept asking her to go out with him. The first time she mentioned him, Grandmother had looked up sharply. "I hope you told him you were a married woman, Jessie."

"I didn't have to tell him. He knows I'm a married woman. But he isn't trying to marry me, Mama. He just wants me to go to the movies with him. I think he's lonely."

"Men always think they're lonely when there's a good-looking woman around," Grandmother pointed out. "Just remember — they're all alike."

Angie looked at her mother soberly. With her cheeks flushed and her chin up she looked almost young. Celia was twelve and her mother was past twenty when Celia was born so she had to be in her thirties, but sometimes she looked like a young girl.

A couple of evenings afterward Angie heard her mother and her grandmother talking in the loud angry voices that didn't even care about listening ears. "The trouble is," Angie's mother was storming, "I'm not married and I'm not divorced, but I'm not dead yet either. I'm still young, Mama, and I'm not ready to sit in a rocking chair and watch the world go by."

"I know exactly what you're talking about," Grandmother said more quietly. "I'm not sixty until next March, and I know as well as you how hard it is to feel that life is passing you by, but you have two little girls to think about, Jessie."

There was a long silence, and then Angie heard

her mother say something about getting a divorce. Divorce was a nasty word as far as Grandmother was concerned. The quarrel went on for a long time, but for once Angie's mother won the argument, and the next night Jeff Granger came to the house to meet the family and take Angie's mother out to a movie.

He brought a big box of candy for Grandmother and Celia and Angie. Grandmother was still stiff, but she was polite and asked him to come in and sit down while he waited for Angie's mother to finish dressing.

Angie was watching television and she tried to make herself as small as possible so he wouldn't notice her, but after he had talked for a while to Grandmother and Celia he came and leaned over her chair. "You must be Angie," he said in a coaxing voice. "Hello, Angie."

"Hello," she muttered faintly.

"I'm Jeff. Jeff Granger. I'm a friend of your mother's." He held out his hand and she put hers into it. Immediately his strong fingers closed, holding her hand a prisoner. "So you are Angie. I've been wanting to meet you for a long time. We have a lot to talk about, you and I."

She felt as helpless as a bird hypnotized by a snake. He was a stranger, and yet she knew him; his grip on her hand was warm and friendly, and yet she felt cold. Angie was glad her mother came into the room at that moment, and Jeff Granger released her hand and turned away.

After they had gone Angie sat quietly in her chair, not really seeing the figures on television, not really hearing her grandmother and Celia talking about Jeff Granger.

"I think he's nice," Celia declared, her mouth half-filled with chocolate. "Did you like him, Angie?"

"No," Angie said.

Her grandmother looked at her sharply, then she carefully laid aside the woolen strips she was braiding into a rug. "Why, Angie? Why don't you like him?"

Angie wet her lips nervously. She knew what her grandmother wanted; she wanted Angie to say something shocking about the man. That he was married . . . that he had a long police record . . . that he had a bad reputation with the ladies, anything that Grandmother could hold to and believe and offer as proof positive that he was an evil person. Because Grandmother really believed the things that Angie said. She protested a lot, but she believed.

"I don't know," she said, aware that both Grandmother and Celia were watching her closely. "I just know . . . I know that he is going to be someone important to us. He's going to be here for a long time."

"You mean Mama's going to marry him?" Celia prompted.

"No. No, I don't think she'll do that."

"Well, I should hope not," Grandmother said sharply. "If you ask *me*, he'll be here today and gone tomorrow. That type jumps around a lot."

Angie wanted to protest. She wanted to point out that Jeff was not so much interested in her mother as he was in her. That Angie and her strange gift were what drew him, and Angie who would hold him until . . . until . . .

She shook her head clearing away the shadowy

images she didn't really want to see. More and more often she learned that she could do so. Close her mind and her heart to the things she didn't want to know, the truths she didn't want to admit.

She went to bed early that night. Her grandmother thought she had a headache and suggested an aspirin, but Angie knew she didn't need an aspirin. She just wanted to lie quietly in her bed and think about her father; in a strange way she wanted this time to say good-bye to her father. Now he had been gone for a year and a half. . . . Perhaps if he knew about Jeff Granger he would try to return. And then she sighed in the darkness, admitting to herself that even this knowledge would not make him come home.

She held up her hand and looked at it, remembering the clasp of her father's hand, seeing again the rare flash of his smile, hearing the deep note of his laughter. Perhaps now that he was no longer burdened with the responsibilities and frustrations of being a husband and father, the laughter came more easily, the smile appeared more frequently.

He was a peace-loving man, her father. He dreamed large dreams, but was content with small realities: a warm bed, a cold drink, and good food under his belt. He would work hard and ask in return only the small comforts and a maximum of tranquility.

Tranquility was a word she had learned from her father. It was a word he used lovingly, and he told Angie that it meant things like faint music and the whirr of crickets and warm sunshine soaking into one's bones. She knew that tranquility was something he had never been able to achieve in his home or his marriage. She hoped he had it now.

She understood only faintly why she was feeling so sad, so lonely for her father. If her father had stayed with them, she might have gone on being a child for years and years. Her father knew she was different, but he was content to leave Angie alone. Jeff Granger wouldn't be content.

She slept at last, but her dreams were troubled and she wakened when she heard a car door open and close, the sound of quickly muted laughter, and then the tapping of her mother's footsteps crossing the porch. She knew her mother would be smiling as she tiptoed into her bedroom and undressed in the dark so she wouldn't disturb Grandmother. Her mother smiled a lot these days, for the first time since Stacy had left them, since Angie's father had gone away.

Her grandmother was probably lying awake too and feeling the same nostalgic sadness that Angie was feeling. There was a curious bond between Angie and her grandmother. Neither of them talked about it, but both were painfully aware that it was there. If Grandmother had her way, the road ahead for Angie would be uncomplicated by the strange gift that burdened her days and haunted her dreaming.

She turned her face against the pillow and felt the tears press against her eyelids. Her father seemed very close, but her heart told her that he was half a world away.

FOUR

Jeff came to the house often. Sometimes he took Angie's mother out to dinner or to a movie, and on rare occasions they went dancing. Grandmother stopped protesting. At least, she stopped arguing in front of the children, but the hostility was still there, and Angie could feel it.

Angie sometimes wished that she could reassure her grandmother, that she could promise her that all the things she feared — the divorce, the remarriage — would never come about. And watching her mother bloom and glow under Jeff's attentions, she couldn't help being glad.

There was nothing Jeff said or did that should have made Angie tense and anxious, but she couldn't dismiss the feeling that he was waiting —

watching her and waiting. He was nice to all of them. He was almost objectionably polite to Grandmother, and he teased Celia and brought her small presents, but he never tried to make Angie like him. He wouldn't bribe her with flattery or special attentions. If he felt the special bond between them, he was apparently willing to wait until Angie acknowledged it. Sometimes she almost forgot that she had been afraid of him.

One Saturday he came and took her and Celia to the zoo. They were really too old to go to the zoo, and Celia grew bored quickly. She wanted to go on the rides, so Jeff bought her a whole roll of tickets.

"Do you want to ride, Angie?" he asked, and she shook her head quickly.

"No," she said. "I'll just watch."

"She's a sissy," Celia said.

Jeff didn't agree or disagree; he just gave Celia the tickets, and then followed Angie to a bench where they sat down to watch. It was a fall day, but the sun was pleasantly warm on their backs. A tranquil day, Angie thought sadly.

Jeff looked at her unsmiling. "You used to be afraid of me," he said at last. "You aren't now."

She answered him gravely. "No, not now . . ."

He didn't ask questions, but she could see that he was pleased.

When Celia had used up the roll of tickets she came back, and they walked around looking at all the animals in their cages. "They hate to be caged up," Angie said. "If someone unlocked all the cages some night, I bet they wouldn't even run away. They just want to know they can get out if they feel like it."

"You're crazy," Celia told her witheringly. "If those cages weren't locked, the animals would be all over the city, killing people and probably eating them. I suppose you'd like to have something like *that* happen."

"I don't think they'd kill anyone. I bet they'd keep as far away from people as they could get. Look at that brown bear. He'd be perfectly happy to find a big park and climb a tree and live on honey and nuts. Bears are supposed to live like that."

Jeff grinned. "Honey, your ideas are pretty sound."

He took both their hands when they crossed a main thoroughfare, but afterward he forgot to drop Angie's hand. She wanted to pull away, but she was reluctant to hurt his feelings. After a while Jeff seemed to sense something was wrong, and he let her hand go and reached for his wallet so he could buy peanuts for the monkeys.

It was a relaxed pleasant day, but as the shadows deepened Angie felt a small warning bell in her subconscious begin ringing. "Could we go home now, Jeff? Right now?"

He looked at her questioningly. "If you like, Angie. . ."

"I don't want to go home," Celia objected. "We haven't been to the snake house yet. I want to see the snakes."

They stood there, Jeff looking helplessly from one to the other. "Tell you what," he said at last. "We'll go home now and come back again next Saturday. How about that?"

"I want to see the snakes," Celia repeated stubbornly.

"We can't. We have to go home right now."

Angie spoke so quickly that both of them looked at her in amazement.

They got into Jeff's car, and he turned out into the stream of traffic. Angie sat in the seat against the door, and Celia was wedged into the place beside Jeff. He kept looking over at Angie worriedly. "Angie, you're so pale. You aren't sick, are you?"

"No." She wet her lips carefully. "But mother is."

When they arrived at the house, Angie hurried up the walk and pounded on the door. After what seemed an eternity her grandmother opened it. "Sakes alive, child, you don't have to hammer the house down. I was upstairs putting some towels away. . . ." She broke off as Angie brushed past her into the living room.

"Where's Mother?" Angie asked. "Is she home from work yet?"

"No, she's late. Should have been here twenty minutes ago." Grandmother looked at Celia and then Jeff. "What is it?"

"Angie says mother is sick," Celia declared ghoulishly. "She might have been in an accident. She might even be dead. . . ."

"Be quiet, Celia," her grandmother said. "March upstairs and get washed for dinner the pair of you. I never heard such hysterical foolishness. You mother will probably be here before I carve the pot roast." She looked past the two children at Jeff. "You can stay for dinner if you don't mind pot luck."

The invitation was the first really civil gesture Grandmother had extended to Jeff. She must have been really terrified to make an exception now.

When the girls came back downstairs, Jeff was aimlessly twirling the dial of the radio and Grandmother was standing where she could watch the bus stop on the street corner.

"I've told her she shouldn't work all day Saturday, even if she does get time and a half. She needs that day with her children. But no, she wants to save money ahead for a vacation and Lord knows what all. . . ." Grandmother stopped talking abruptly as Jeff got the newscast, but there was no word of an accident, nothing but war news and another message from the President.

The hands of the clock crawled past six thirty, past seven and seven thirty, past eight.

"If she isn't home in half an hour, I'll call the police," Grandmother said every few minutes.

"What will you tell them?" Jeff asked softly. "That your daughter, a woman in her thirties, is late home from work?"

Grandmother looked helpless. She knew as well as any of them that the police would be unimpressed by the premonitions of a girl not yet eleven years old.

No one wanted to eat, but at nine o'clock Grandmother ushered all of them in to the table. "This is utter nonsense," she scolded. "We'll sit down and have our dinner. She could walk in the door any minute."

Angie was sure she couldn't eat a bite, but when her grandmother placed a heaping plate before her she found that her appetite had been miraculously restored. She looked across at Jeff. "Mother's all right now," she said. "You'd better eat your dinner."

Jeff and her grandmother exchanged quick

glances, and then her grandmother went to look out the window for perhaps the hundredth time.

In just a few moments the telephone rang, and Jeff leaped to answer it. "Where are you?" he asked. "What happened? We've been frantic. Angie got this idea that something was wrong while we were at the zoo and . . ." He stopped and listened for a long time, and after a while he hung up and came back to the table.

"Angie was right," he said. "She's all right now. She's coming home in a cab."

"Why a cab?" Grandmother snapped. "What happened? Is she hurt?"

"You could say she's a little upset," Jeff said mildly. "One of the elevators jammed, and the auxiliary power didn't snap on. Jessie was pretty panicky; she says she hates closed places anyway."

"How long was she stuck in the elevator?" Grandmother wanted to know. "When did it happen?"

"When she started home," Jeff said softly. "About the time Angie insisted we leave the zoo." He sat down, picked up his coffee cup, and took a long sip.

Angie's mother drove up in a matter of minutes. Now that the danger was past she was flushed and gay about her adventure. "Imagine! Six of us cooped up in that thing for over three hours. The building superintendent was delighted to send all of us home in cabs. I almost passed out when I realized we were stuck. I can't stand to be cooped up, you know that, Mama. Remember that time at school when that horrid boy locked me in the closet and I fainted. . . ."

Grandmother was looking not at Jessie but at

Angie, and her eyes were very grave. "You didn't have any cake, Angie," she said.

Jeff leaned up against the doorframe watching all of them. He didn't say anything, but his eyes were dark with excitement.

When Grandmother said it had been a big day and the girls should go to bed, only Celia protested. Angie was bone tired all of a sudden. But she remembered her manners and shook hands with Jeff, thanking him for taking them to the zoo.

"That's okay, honey," he said. "We'll do it again. Lots of times."

When she was in bed and long after Celia was asleep, she could still hear her mother and grandmother and Jeff talking. Occasionally her grandmother's voice rose, but then she would be quiet again.

"Your grandmother is an old blister," she remembered her father telling her, "but she really loves you, Angie. She'll always want what's right for you. So if the time ever comes when you have to make any tough decisions. . ."

Angie closed her eyes and let the faraway voices fade out. Ten and a half was pretty young to make tough decisions.

Grandmother went to her guild meeting on Wednesday evening. And on that night Jeff came to the house to talk to Angie and her mother. He entered and took off his coat and tossed it across a chair as if he meant to stay a long time. They sat in the living room just like grown-ups who are discussing business.

"Angie, I want to talk to you. Talk to you seri-

54

ously about this gift of yours." He turned his head and looked at her directly. "ESP isn't a new thing, but people are very excited by it, and there's nothing wrong with it. That's what you have to understand. Even in the Bible certain people had gifts of prophecy. Sometimes they took the form of dreams, but it was always some special person who had this gift. I think you have it. You know you have it, and it scares you. Right?"

She looked at him and nodded.

"You're just a little kid. But maybe I can make you understand. You could earn a great deal of money, Angie. Enough so your mother and grandmother and sister would be comfortable for as long as they live. You'd like to have a nice place to live and a new car and be able to take vacations whenever you felt like it. You'd like that, wouldn't you?"

She nodded again, pushing aside the shadowy images that wouldn't come clear, trying hard to concentrate on his words.

"Angie, do you believe I want what is best for you?"

"Yes," she said without hesitation.

"All right, this is my idea. Do you suppose you could get these vibrations when you want to or do you have to wait for them to come?"

She thought about the question for a moment, remembering that her mother had asked almost the same thing. "Sometimes I can see pictures when I want to, but most of the time I just know."

"Would you be willing to try some experiments?"

She looked at her mother, who hadn't said a

word, who was relaxed and easy in her chair, her eyes moving from Jeff to her daughter and then back to Jeff again.

"I guess so. . . ."

"Fine." He sat down on the edge of the table and folded his arms. "Now don't look at your mother, Angie. Close your eyes, if you like, and just think about this for a moment. Okay?" He was quiet for a space of half a dozen heartbeats, and then he spoke again. "Now your mother has something in her hand. Think hard and see if you can tell me what it is."

Angie thought hard, but nothing happened. She opened her eyes and smiled at him. "It doesn't work," she said clearly. "I didn't think of anything."

Her mother smiled too and held up both hands. They were empty.

"Let's try again," Jeff said softly. "Let's try again, sweetheart."

She closed her eyes obediently. A nostalgic sadness filled her, and she thought about Stacy. From across the room she could almost feel her mother thinking about Stacy. She could see the plump witless little face . . . the pudgy aimlessly waving fist. . . .

"It's something that belonged to Stacy," she said without opening her eyes. "Stacy's ring. . . ."

Her mother started to cry, and Jeff came over to hug her. Both of them turned and looked at Angie.

"You see, you *can* do it," Jeff exulted. "I don't care if it's part mental telepathy, part hocus-pocus, and part witchcraft. We're in, sweetheart." He whirled about and went to pick up his overcoat, returned with a small metal truck, which he put into Angie's hands.

"What do you get from this, honey?"

She turned it over, and then looked up at him doubtfully. "It isn't yours. It belonged to a little boy who . . . who lives a long way from here. Only he's bigger now. He's bigger than Celia. He's your boy."

Jeff leaned over and took the truck out of her hands and returned it to his pocket. "Yes," he said ."He's bigger now. He's my boy."

They tried other things. Her mother held a coin, a brooch, a pen. None of them came through to Angie, although she was really trying. And then Jeff said, "What is your mother holding now, Angie?"

She answered without hesitation, "My father's key ring. He left it on the table the night he went away."

She was exhausted after that first session, and her grandmother was furious when she came home, but there was nothing she could do about it.

"You'll have to learn a bunch of signals," Jeff told her the next time they worked together. "We hope you won't need them, but we have to play it safe. So when I start off by saying *Angie*, that means the article I'm holding belongs to a man. If I say *honey* or *sweetheart* or *sugar*, the article belongs to a woman. If I say *I have here*, the article is metal. . . ."

"But that's cheating, isn't it?" Angie's mother interrupted.

"Nope, that's showmanship," Jeff replied cheerfully. "Let's try it, shall we?"

Rehearsing was almost like a game. First she learned the signals, and then she stored them in her memory. Sometimes she delighted Jeff by answering his questions even before he gave the signals. Sometimes she was utterly cold, nothing happened; she just tensed up and couldn't think. During one of these times Jeff said she ought to take tranquilizers; they would help her to relax. At first Angie's mother said she'd never hear of such a thing. Of course, they wouldn't start giving her drugs. But Jeff just laughed, and sometime afterward he gave Angie the white pills that made her feel a little sleepy.

The strange thing was that the more she played the game — learning signals, counterplotting — the less she was liable to be troubled by the unsought visions that had come to her for as long as she could remember. Her mother still kept a journal and carefully recorded everything, but the entries were less and less frequent as time went on.

It was a dreamlike world she moved in. She went to school, she played hopscotch and worked on posters for the art fair, she talked to her grandmother and her mother and Celia, but only when Jeff was there teaching her, working with her, did she really feel alive and important.

"You two make me think of Trilby and Svengali," Angie's mother said once, when she was cross about being ignored. "How long is this going on before we start getting some action?"

Jeff walked over and patted her cheek. "Patience, sweetheart. We don't want to blow it, do we?"

That night they stopped the session early, and Jeff and Angie's mother went to dinner and a night-club. The next day she was her cheerful self again.

A few weeks later Jeff announced that Angie was going on TV. "It's an early-morning show, one of those personality-in-the-news shows. She won't be paid very much, but she'll probably get a lot of attention. People will start talking about her; they'll want to have her answer questions. It could lead to almost anything."

"But what will I do?" Angie asked. "What am I supposed to do?"

"That's the joker. We don't know. The master of ceremonies is rigging up something just to prove to himself that I'm on the level. In case the thing falls flat, we'll have something rehearsed — a plant who'll look real in the studio audience."

Angie long ago had stopped trying to figure out what Jeff was talking about. She only knew that she wanted him to be pleased with her. She also wanted her mother to be happy, and her mother was happy as long as Jeff was around.

Going on television was a frightening experience, but not as scary as if she had been alone. Jeff was right there beside her, and her mother was seated in the audience. The master of ceremonies was a thin young man who bounced around a lot and made jokes, but he was serious when he introduced Angie. "Our next guest is a young lady new to television. To look at her we could assume that she is new to almost everything. How old are you, Angie?"

Jeff's elbow nudged her, and she spoke up in a frightened squeak. "I'm ten. . . . I'm going on eleven."

"I've been talking to a lot of people about you, Angie — your teachers, your family, the woman who runs a CYO camp you attended last summer — and all of them say the same thing. Do you know what they say?"

"They say that I know things that have happened . . . and things that are going to happen." This part had been rehearsed, and Angie felt a little uncomfortable saying the words. "Just like I can tell you what you had for breakfast this morning."

"Go on!" The interviewer sounded incredulous. "Can you really?"

"Yes, you had soft-boiled eggs."

"Amazing," the man said. "Can you really look into my mind and see that, Angie?"

"No, sir, I can't," she said. "But I can see the spot on your tie."

The audience laughed, and the breaking-in part was over. The man explained that Angie's performance wasn't a gag, that various members of the audience had been invited to ask a question of Angie by writing it out and handing it in. The slips of paper were signed, and each person was asked to stand when he or she recognized the question so that the vibrations would be clearer. This part of the act had been rehearsed too. A woman in the audience had submitted a question that Angie would be able to answer fluently, but Angie wouldn't use it unless. . . .

The slips of paper were handed to Angie, but she didn't try to read them. It was very quiet in the studio as she held them in her hand, waiting . . . waiting.

The intent faces of the people in the audience bothered her so she closed her eyes, and after a while she spoke in a very small voice. "There was a fire," she said at last. "A big fire."

She thought about the fire for a moment while the silence ticked. . . . "Not like a forest fire or a house fire but a big fire *in* something. . . ."

"Like an incinerator?" a voice prompted, and Angie nodded. She knew about incinerators. There was one at school.

"Yes, like that. The money wasn't buried in the garden. It was in a glove. It was in a glove she used when she was gardening. She thought someone would find it after she died. But . . . someone, a woman, sent all the old clothes away and they were burned. And the money was burned too."

She was aware of the stir in the audience, and she opened her eyes to the sight of Jeff's reassuring grin.

The woman who stood on her feet was pale, and she was looking at Angie curiously. The master of ceremonies found the correct slip and read the question to the audience. "Can you tell me where my Aunt Charlotte buried her money before she died."

"Would you like to try another one, honey?" the master of ceremonies asked, and then turned to the audience. "Would you like to have this remarkable young woman answer another question?" The applause was thunderous. Obediently Angie took the papers in her hands.

"You want to know if you're going to get that job you've been waiting for. It has something to do with airplanes," she began easily, and then her voice faltered. She put the papers down hastily. "I guess I'm tired," she said in a shaking voice. "No, no you won't get the job . . . I'm sorry."

She had to sit there while they found the slip with the question, but she couldn't bear to look at the young man who rose to his feet and admitted to having submitted the question.

Angie was glad when the show was over, and they were in Jeff's car driving home.

"There, that wasn't so bad, was it?" her mother said happily. "And just think, honey, I would have to work over a week to earn that much money."

"If she hadn't come up with that story about the incinerator, there wouldn't have been *any* money," Jeff said grimly. "This was strictly on speculation. But next time . . ." He turned and looked at Angie gravely. "Now what was all that about the young fellow not getting his job?"

Angie was silent for a moment. "I just don't think he'll get it."

"You know he won't get the job," Jeff said. "Why, Angie?"

She could feel herself shaking, but she kept her voice steady. "He'll be in an accident. He's going to be killed." Tears welled into her eyes, but she blinked them away. "I should have told him to be careful."

Her mother put her arm around Angie's shoulder and patted her. "Honey, you could be mistaken. Don't you remember when Sister Gertrude was sick, and you said she'd get better. She died the very next day. And you told Mrs. Nance that Carla's leg would be fine, but she still has her braces, and now the doctors think they might have to amputate."

Angie turned her face against her mother's sleeve and continued to weep.

Her grandmother was stony-faced and angry at the dinner table that evening, even though Jeff hadn't stayed for dinner, but had rushed off to attend to some business.

"Just look at her! She looks like a little ghost," Grandmother declared, pointing a shaking finger at Angie. "All this conniving and rehearsing and tampering with a God-given gift. No good will come of it, you'll see."

"Mother, it isn't hurting her. It's insuring her future. Our future. If Angie gets on big-time TV, we'll all be rich. Don't you want to be able to stop worrying about next year and the year after that? I do. And Angie does. And Jeff wants it for us."

Grandmother's lips tightened, the way they always did when Jeff's name was mentioned. "That's another thing," she said. "You're always saying Jeff this and Jeff that. What has he to do with Angie or she with him? Angie is our child."

"Angie is *my* child," Angie's mother corrected her. "I'm the one who will decide what's best for her."

Of course, they made up the quarrel before they went to bed, but it was upsetting all the same, and Angie's sleep was broken by dreams of a car that crashed and shattered and burned.

FIVE

For a week nothing happened. Jeff didn't come to the house, although he talked to Angie's mother on the phone. Angie went to school as usual, and several of the children told her their mothers had seen her on the TV show. Everyone was more interested in the large amount of money Angie had been paid than in her performance.

"My mother says it's a trick. That anyone can do it," one unpleasant child told her with shattering honesty.

"It isn't a trick at all," Angie said. And then she remembered the signals she had learned so painstakingly. She remembered the woman who had been planted in the audience in case her mind went blank. "Well, we practice things like that, but it isn't a cheating trick."

On Tuesday evening, just before bedtime, Jeff called and asked Angie to stay home from school the next day. He wanted her to watch tomorrow's program of the show she had been on. It was important.

Her mother agreed readily enough, but her grandmother stubbornly refused. "What's more important than Angie getting an education, I'd like to know? And to watch a stupid TV show, of all things. Jeff is trying to crack the whip to see how high we'll jump, that's all. I say that Angie should get up and go to school in the morning."

Angie's mother shrugged. "I have to agree with you, Mama, about her education being important, but Jeff is thinking of Angie's career. I think we should do as he asks."

"What career?" Grandmother demanded. "One appearance on a TV show can hardly be considered a career."

"She does have a career, though. The show was just the beginning. Yesterday I went to the lawyer's office and signed the paper making Jeff her agent. That means he'll accept engagements, handle contracts, and take care of all the business details. If her work involves travel, she'll have a tutor go along and teach her. It's some kind of law, the lawyer says. . . ."

"You mean you did all this without even talking it over with the rest of us?" Grandmother sounded mad and hurt at the same time.

"I knew you'd have a million objections," Angie's mother said calmly. "I knew you'd start trying to ruin everything. The trouble with you, Mama, is that you hate men. Not just some men, but *all* men."

"And you don't; that's pretty obvious." Grandmother spoke in a hard furious voice. "Just because a man sweet-talks you, you're ready to let him lead you around like a lapdog on a leash."

Angie slipped out of the room, but she didn't go upstairs. Instead she let herself out of the house and sat on the back porch in the friendly darkness. She was sorry that her mother and her grandmother were mad at each other, but skipping school tomorrow would be nice. Miss Pilgrim pressed hard on arithmetic, which was Angie's worst subject. She sat there with her knees hugged up to her chin and her arms wrapped around her bare legs until Celia came looking for her.

"Grandmother says you'd better get to bed if you don't want to catch more trouble than you can handle," she announced fiercely. Then, as Angie got to her feet, offering no objection, she dropped the threatening tone and asked curiously, "What's Grandma so mad about and why's Mama crying, do you know?"

"You'd better ask Grandma," Angie said, knowing that Celia wouldn't dare.

The next morning Angie didn't go to school. No one called her at the usual time so she curled back under the blankets. No one called Celia either. When they finally went down to breakfast, Grandma only said that what was sauce for one goose was sauce for the other. The announcement didn't make sense to either of the girls, but they were both so impressed at having an unexpected day off that they didn't ask any questions.

Jeff arrived about fifteen minutes before the show started, and he and Angie's mother had a brief, hurried consultation in the kitchen. Grandmother was glum and silent, which wasn't like her.

When the program came on, they all watched it. Angie had the warm friendly feeling that the bouncy young man on the television screen was a friend of hers. Celia squirmed in her chair, not really interested but captured by the sense that something important was about to take place that she shouldn't miss.

Grandmother rocked in her chair and said nothing, not even when Angie's mother asked her if she'd like a cup of coffee. Jeff perched on the edge of the table and drank his coffee. Once he winked at Angie, a boyish wink that seemed to make them conspirators. "You and I know that all this feuding and fussing isn't going to make a bit of difference," the wink said. "You and I, Angie. . ."

At the very end of the program the master of ceremonies, who had been laughing and telling jokes one after another, was suddenly completely serious.

"We have had letters," he said. "And we have had telephone calls, and a few people have even walked up to me on the street to ask about a guest who visited the show a little over a week ago. You may have seen the program or been a member of the audience. Or you may have heard about it and been curious. On October twelfth we introduced a very young lady who is probably destined to be one of the leading mentalists of our time. This amazing child answered questions submitted by the studio audience. A young man asked about a job he had applied for, and Angie told him that he wouldn't get the job. We all sensed that Angie was very upset, but not until after the program did she confide the reason she had told the young man he would not get the position. He would die in an automobile accident."

The master of ceremonies paused effectively, and then went on. "Last evening the papers carried an account of the accident and the death of one Arthur Mason Holden, the same young man who had been in the studio and submitted a question to ten-year-old Angie Scofield on October twelfth . . . of this year. . . ."

The program went off, and a commercial flashed on the screen. Grandmother looked at Angie sharply. "Is this true? Did it happen the way the man said?"

"Yes," Angie replied. "Only, only I didn't tell *him* the man was going to die. I told Jeff and Mother."

Jeff leaned forward. "I went right back to the studio and told Stew what Angie had said. He was interested enough in the information to follow through on it. I don't know how they got the fellow's name and did the rundown on him. But yesterday Stew called, and then I got a call from Los Angeles offering us a show out there the day after this story hits the papers. How about that?" He turned to Angie then. "How about it, sugar? You'd like to fly out to California, wouldn't you? Disneyland, Marineland, lots of movie stars. . ."

Angie nodded. Celia started bouncing up and down. "Are we all going, Jeff?"

He looked at Angie's mother and her grandmother. "I guess it depends on what the family wants to do."

"It seems a long way to travel for one national TV appearance," Angie's mother said slowly. "Certainly I don't think all the family should go."

"I can make all the necessary arrangements for you and Angie to fly out," Jeff told her. He looked around at all of them, and Angie knew that he was really trying to sell the idea to her grandmother.

"Couldn't you come, too?" Angie's mother asked. "You're Angie's agent. Won't it look funny if you aren't there?"

"Not as funny as it would look if I went," Jeff said. "Look, here is a little girl with a remarkable gift of prevision. The master of ceremonies will talk to the child's mother and learn that this sort of thing has been going on for years. The program will be set — not that we'll feed Angie any questions and answers — but we want to make sure she doesn't fall flat on her face. It will be a breeze, and afterward Angie can write her own ticket." He reached over and patted Angie's hand. "Or Jeff can write it for her."

Grandmother leaned back in her chair and started rocking slowly, back and forth. Her eyes weren't angry anymore, but they were frightened.

"Come here, Angie," she said at last, and held out her hand. Angie came forward slowly until she was standing directly in front of her grandmother. Their eyes were almost level. "Tell me, Angie," she said. "You're the one who's supposed to see what lies ahead. Is this the sort of life you really want? Will it make you happy? Will it be good for your mother and for Celia? Never mind about me. I'm an old woman, and I don't matter that much. But what about you, Angie? Will it make you happy?"

Angie wanted to fling herself into her grandmother's bony arms and weep. She wanted to weep for the loss of her childhood, and she wanted to weep for her mother, who wouldn't be happy no matter which road Angie chose to follow. She had never lied to her grandmother, not about anything important. "I don't know if it will make me happy, but I know it's what we're going to do, Grandmother."

The next few days were hurried and strange. Her mother went to the school and made arrangements for Angie to be away until the next Monday. Angie wasn't even allowed to say good-bye to Miss Pilgrim or any of her friends. Instead she worked with Jeff the two evenings before they flew to Los Angeles for the show.

"I wish you could be there, Jeff," she said once. "I'll be scared without you."

He looked at her, smiling faintly, and all at once she knew. "Jeff, you will be there, won't you?"

"I'll fly out after you," he told her. "But it's our secret, Angie. You won't tell your mother?"

"Not if you don't want me to," she said soberly. "She'd be glad if she knew you were going to be there with us, Jeff."

"I know." He sounded tired, and she could tell he didn't want to talk about the trip anymore.

Angie's mother had her hair cut short and styled in a new way, but Jeff told her not to dare cut Angie's hair. "Let it grow — the longer the better

— and don't worry too much about the shadows under her eyes. They give her that mysterious quality. And don't forget the pills in case she tenses up. . . ."

All these last-minute instructions were delivered as they waited at the airport. Grandmother and Celia had stayed home. Grandmother had finally bowed to the will of the majority, but she still wasn't happy about the trip.

"I don't think she should be taking those pills," Angie's mother said unhappily. "What's in them anyway? You never did tell me."

"They're tranquilizers, sweetie, and I *have* told you, again and again, that they won't hurt Angie. You can try them out yourself. Take one tonight just before you go to bed. It will make you feel relaxed, and for a half hour or so your mind will be clear as a bell. Then you'll be able to close your eyes and sleep like a baby."

Angie's mother looked at him thoughtfully. "All right, I'll try one," she said at last. "But I warn you, Jeff. If I feel the least bit high, or get the slightest hint of depression, I won't give them to Angie. Agreed?"

"Agreed," he said, and leaned forward to drop a swift kiss on her cheek. "Better hustle. They just called your plane. Now relax and have fun. Someone will meet you as you get off the plane, and everything is taken care of." He walked to the ramp with them, and then handed over the bag Angie's mother would keep with her on the plane. "Be good, you gals. I'll be thinking about you every minute." He put his hand on Angie's head and patted it gently. "Knock 'em dead, sweetheart."

"We'll see you Sunday," Angie's mother reminded him. "You won't forget to meet the plane?"

"I won't forget," he said, and winked at Angie.

Angie's mother turned to give the man their tickets, and Jeff whipped a large dark moustache from his pocket and held it below his nose. Angie giggled because he looked so funny, but when her mother turned her head the moustache was back in Jeff's pocket.

The plane trip was exciting. Angie had never flown before, but she wasn't afraid. She sat in a window seat and looked down at the view of the city slipping and sliding away from her.

Her mother immediately started talking to a woman across the aisle, wanting to make sure that the people on the plane knew that Angie was flying to Los Angeles to appear on a national television show. Angie looked through the window and tried to shut out the sound of her mother's voice. When the stewardess came to see if she wanted some Coke or a glass of milk, Angie shook her head and said that she wasn't hungry, thank you. Her mother had coffee and a little later she had a cocktail. She was having a wonderful time.

The plane climbed up and up and up, until there was nothing to see but padded clouds drifting below. The clouds looked like fat awkward sheep, Angie told herself. She must remember to tell Miss Pilgrim about them.

The stewardess brought their dinner. She was a pretty young woman, who smiled at Angie as if they were the same age, instead of a child and an adult. Angie smiled back at her, recognizing immediately a kindred spirit.

"Is it fun being a stewardess?" she asked shyly, as the young woman snapped her tray into place. "Is it more fun than being a secretary or a school-teacher or a mother?"

The girl laughed. "I guess I'm not qualified to say, since I've never been any of those other things. Why? Would you like to be a stewardess some-day?"

Angie thought about the question, and then shook her head regretfully. "No, I guess not. Jeff wouldn't like it."

The stewardess looked surprised. "Is Jeff your boyfriend?"

"No," Angie said. "He's my agent."

A stout businesslike man met them at the air-port. In the taxi going into town he told Angie's mother that their room was ready at the hotel and that he'd left a call for eight thirty the next morn-ing.

"The show doesn't go on until eleven, but you'll want to have your breakfast and be ready when the car picks you up at ten. Is that agreeable?"

"Then tomorrow evening Jackie will want to take you out to dinner. You and Angie. There may be some publicity pictures. I've already cleared it with Jeff. Agreeable?"

Angie sat in her corner of the cab and thought what a boring man he was. She was glad when they arrived at the hotel and finally escaped to their room.

Angie's mother was thrilled with the room, but she didn't act excited until after the bellboy who brought up their suitcases had opened the windows, turned on the lights in the bathroom, and gone away. "Just feel those beds, Angie. And will you look at the bathroom! Wait until I tell Mabel Dunham that we had a glassed-in pink shower. . . ." She ran around like a child — turning on the lamps, peering into the drawers, and switching on the color TV. "Look at the postcards. Aren't they lovely? Would you like to send some postcards, honey?"

"Maybe I'll send one to Miss Pilgrim," Angie said slowly. "I could tell her about the clouds that looked like sheep. And we could write to Grandmother. She'd like to get a postcard."

"Fine. We'll do that. And one for Jeff so he can see what he's missing." Her face clouded a little when she spoke of Jeff. She was still disappointed that he hadn't come along.

Angie was getting sleepy, but her mother wanted to watch TV for a while. "You can go to sleep, sweetie. I'm too excited, I guess."

"Are you scared about tomorrow?" Angie asked, and her mother looked startled for a moment.

"Why no, honey. I'm not scared. I have absolute confidence in you. And you aren't to worry either. Jeff says everything will work out beautifully." She took Angie's face between her hands and smiled at her. "You like Jeff, don't you? I mean *really* like him?" She didn't wait for Angie's answer, but whirled away to adjust the television to another channel. "Maybe I should take one of your tranquilizers. I feel as if I'm walking about eight inches off the ground."

Angie didn't stay awake to see whether he mother took a tranquilizer or not. She fell asleep almost at once and had only the dimmest recollection of her mother moving about the room in her bare feet. "Angie, this rug is as soft as kitten fur." Later she must have called room service for a snack. "Honey, are you sure you wouldn't like a cup of hot chocolate?"

She wasn't worried about the television appearance. Jeff would be there, hiding behind his black moustache probably, but he'd be there. She wouldn't even ask Jeff why he hadn't wanted her mother to know that he was in town. She had an idea she'd be happier not knowing.

SIX

Angie wakened to the unfamiliar sounds of a great hotel stirring slowly to life. Soft footsteps along the corridor, faraway voices and bursts of laughter that were turned on and off by the opening and closing of doors. There was the sound of water running and occasionally the bleat of horns from the traffic fourteen stories down.

For a moment Angie stared wide-eyed at the ceiling. It was a beautiful ceiling with gold flecks dusted into the paint. The realization of where she was touched her, and she sat up in bed. She was in California. Today she was going to be on network television. Somewhere her father might sit down before a TV screen and watch her. Would he notice how much she had grown? Would he like the blue dress? Would he be sorry . . . ? And then, as always, she pushed away the thought of her father, telling herself that she didn't really care.

She looked across at her mother in the other twin bed. Asleep, her mother wore the smooth masklike face of a complete stranger. Her mouth was a little open, and she had some creamy stuff rubbed into the circles around her eyes. At first glance she looked as if she might have been crying.

Almost as if she could feel Angie watching her, her mother's eyes flew open. "Hi," she said, and was wide-awake, as if sleep were a cloak she could shrug off without effort. She sat up and swung her feet over the side of the bed, lifting both arms in a prodigious yawn. "What time is it? Mr. Willoughby said he left a call for eight thirty. Do you suppose they forgot us?"

Angie shook her head. "I don't know. Maybe we should get dressed and go downstairs. There's probably a clock in the restaurant."

Her mother smiled and reached for the bedside telephone. "Good morning," she said. "Could you give me the correct time, please? My watch has stopped."

She listened, said thank you, and replaced the telephone in its cradle. "Seven forty-five. Wouldn't you know it? Just because we can sleep till eight thirty, we're both up with the birds. " She didn't look at all embarrassed about saying that her watch had stopped. Angie wondered why her mother wanted to have the operator think she had a watch.

Her mother switched on the TV and turned the dials until she had an early morning movie. Then she went into the bathroom and started the water in the tub. As she trotted back and forth she chattered happily about what a nice day it was, what a fabulous breakfast they would have. "Mr. Willoughby isn't picking us up until ten. We can go out and see some of the sights. . . ."

Angie sat in the middle of her bed with her knees humped up under the blankets and watched this stranger who was her mother. At home her mother was always busy, and there were Grandmother and Celia and sometimes Jeff.

"This is the first time we've been all alone," Angie said, without knowing she was going to speak. When her mother turned and looked at her in some surprise, she went on, "I mean, it's the first time I can remember that we've been all alone."

Her mother smiled and came over to sit on the edge of her bed. "Honey, you are absolutely right. The last time we were alone was. . ." She paused and bit her lip thoughtfully. "Yes, the last time we were alone you were about this big. It was in the hospital, when you were born. Grandmother was at home taking care of Celia, and your father didn't come in except at visiting hours. We were all alone. I used to talk to you when the nurse brought you in for your feedings. I thought you were the most beautiful baby I had ever seen."

Angie smiled. "Prettier than Celia when she was a baby?"

"Much prettier," her mother said without hesitation. "I'd never tell Celia, of course, but she was a spectacularly ugly baby. Her head came to a point for one thing. . . ." She jumped up then and ran to the bathroom to turn off the water, coming back to the doorway.

"Why don't you watch the movie and just relax while I have my bath? I'm going to soak for a while. I brought some of that bath oil Mr. Hayes gave me for Christmas just to try it out. I'll save some for you."

Mr. Hayes was one of the editors on the paper. He gave all the staff members Christmas gifts. Bath oil for the women, after-shave lotion for the men. Jeff said he probably bought both by the gallon.

Angie curled back into her pillow, but she didn't watch the morning movie. It was an old, old one, judging from the cars that were screeching around corners and the unlikely hemlines on the dresses. She closed her eyes and thought about what she would have for breakfast. Toast and hot chocolate was her favorite combination, but her mother would want her to have something more expensive as long as they wouldn't have to pay for anything. Not the food or the cab fare or the hotel or anything. She thought about Jeff, wondering if he was already in Los Angeles, wondering if she would see him at the studio.

While they were waiting for breakfast in the dining room, a waiter came to the table and asked Angie's mother if she was Mrs. Scofield. He said there was a call for her, and when she started to get up, he said he'd bring the phone. She looked worried for a moment, as though the call might be bad news, but it was only Mr. Willoughby asking if everything was all right and telling her that he would pick them up right on schedule.

"Imagine!" Angie's mother said, when the waiter had gone away with the telephone, and another had brought their breakfast. "Wait until I tell the girls at the office about *this!*"

"Maybe we'll take a trip again," Angie said, biting carefully into a sweet roll. "Jeff says we may travel around a lot."

Angie's mother made a little face. "The only trouble is that you're going to have a tutor travel with you. Jeff and I have talked about it already. He says the last thing we want is to get in trouble with the school authorities."

"What will happen," Angie asked slowly, "if they don't like me? If I can't tell them anything?"

"They'll like you, honey," her mother said. "How could they help it?"

Mr. Willoughby arrived on time and drove them to the television studio.

Everything was strange and exciting. The big building was humming with activity, and no one seemed to pay any attention to Angie and her mother. The fat man delivered them to a tall thin young woman who wore dark glasses and had her hair all piled on top of her head as if she'd just stepped out of a shower.

"Hi, I'm Sally Crewe. So you're Angie," she said in a curiously husky voice. "We've been hearing a lot about you. Tell me, honey. Are you for real?"

Angie's mother was the one who answered. She sounded a little sharp. "What do you mean is she for real? You can see that she's a perfectly normal healthy child."

The woman grinned. "I meant is this mind-reading bit for real. There has to be a gimmick, doesn't there?"

"If there was a gimmick," Angie's mother said, "she wouldn't be here."

Angie wanted to explain that she really wasn't a mind reader; even Jeff had soon discovered that fact. "It's just that sometimes I know things," she would have said. But Sally Crewe was whisking them along one carpeted corridor after another. They went into a room and had something called a voice level. Angie had to talk — just talk naturally, Miss Crewe said — so she recited a poem from the book Grandmother had at home. "It takes a heap o' livin' in a house t' make it home," she recited dutifully, and was surprised that Sally Crewe and the young man who was busily adjusting the dials cracked up with laughter. There was certainly nothing funny about the poem; it was her grandmother's favorite.

Afterward they visited the makeup room, and a thin girl and a fussy young man who wore smocks and called each other pet and darling applied makeup to Angie's face and spread it around. They put stuff on her eyes, too, but they didn't try to do anything to her hair. They just brushed it and sprayed on something that would make it shine under the lights.

A man came and took Angie's mother off to have a cup of coffee while another man talked to Angie. She really wanted to see the whole show, but he told her she was to stay in a room offstage until she was called. Then the master of ceremonies would lead her to a chair, and she would sit down and talk to him.

"What about?" Angie asked, and the man who was interviewing her stared.

"You mean you don't know? No one has coached you?" He looked ready to cry.

"Don't worry," Angie said quickly. "I'll think of something. People usually ask me something, and then I try to tell them. That's all."

The man looked unconvinced.

"Why don't you ask me something?" Angie said. "Like . . . about your family." She stopped. "No, I guess you couldn't do that. You don't have a family, do you? Not even a father and mother."

He continued staring at her and his face got red. He pushed back his chair and got up so suddenly that it almost toppled.

The man went away leaving the door open, and Angie could hear the applause that greeted the beginning of the show and the two acts that came on afterward. She could hear singing and laughter and bursts of applause, and she began to wonder why her mother hadn't come back. Maybe she was still having coffee and didn't realize the time almost had come for Angie to go on.

A head popped in the doorway. It was Miss Crewe, looking rushed and worried. "Okay, doll, you're on."

Angie got to her feet obediently and followed Miss Crewe to the place behind the big silken draperies. It was warm; under the lights it would be warmer than ever. Angie was glad she was wearing her lightweight blue dress.

She heard more talking and applause and then her name. Miss Crewe gave her a little nudge, and she stepped between the curtains into the spotlight.

The noise and the whispers seemed to stop as suddenly as if a door had closed, shutting her off from the people who were dimly outlined in the audience.

She stood quietly for a second, waiting for her eyes to adjust to the brightness, waiting for someone to tell her what to do. Only the cameras seemed to be alive, moving up on her slowly and noiselessly, backing away again. A red light blinked on and then off. Another camera turned toward her, its single eye blinking.

A firm hand reached for hers and led her toward a circle of people and a vacant seat. When she sat down and slid back in the chair, her feet didn't quite reach the floor. She smoothed out her dress and waited.

"We've heard so much about you, Angie," the man said. "You'll forgive me if I say it's a shock to see that you're just a regular little girl."

A pretty woman who looked vaguely familiar leaned forward from the circle of people and smiled at Angie. "That's all he knows about it, Angie. There aren't any regular little girls. Each is unique. Right?"

Angie felt her heart skip with excitement. "I know you," she said. "I saw you in the movies. I saw you just last week in a movie on television."

There was laughter from the audience and laughter from the movie star.

The man asked her a few questions about her family and school, and then he asked her if she'd like to answer some questions from people in the audience.

Angie looked out at the audience. She was surprised to see that her mother was in the front row, sitting with the man who had taken her out to buy her coffee. She turned back to the man and smiled. "I'll try. . . ."

"Do you need any special props, Angie? Would you like to have us dim the lights or anything?"

She thought for a moment. "No," she said, "because then I couldn't see."

There was a man in the audience with a microphone. He walked up the aisle and spoke to a man who raised his hand. The page gave him the microphone.

"Your name, sir?"

"Belino, Thomas Belino," the man replied.

"Mr. Belino, would you be so kind as to tell the audience whether you are acquainted with the young lady on the stage? Stand up, please, so they can see you. Now, Mr. Belino . . ."

The man got to his feet. Angie leaned forward to see his face. She wasn't conscious of moving toward the front of the stage. Her response was involuntary.

"Thank you, sir. Now your question, Mr. Belino."

Angie spoke clearly. "Please, don't make him stand up. He's been very sick. He just got out of the hospital."

There was a shocked silence. Mr. Belino sat down, but his eyes never left Angie's face.

"I guess you wanted to ask me whether you're going back to the hospital," Angie said slowly, speaking directly to Mr. Belino, as if the two of them were alone. "Well, everything will be fine. And next summer, I think it's in the summer, you'll be on a big ship, going across the ocean."

There was a buzz from the audience. Angie stood quietly looking around her. Her mother was smiling proudly, and in the opposite corner of the studio she could see Jeff. Even with the moustache and jaunty beard he looked like Jeff.

The man with the microphone found another person with a question for Angie. "Can you tell me where I lost my watch, Angie?"

She thought hard, but couldn't seem to feel anything. "Is it all right if I come down there?" she asked, and without waiting for permission stepped down the four steps into the audience and walked up the aisle. The man with the microphone looked startled and so did the woman who had asked the question.

Angie held out her hand, and after a second's hesitation the woman shook it limply. "I don't think you lost your watch. I think it was stolen." She thought for a moment, and then continued, "I think you *know* it was stolen, and you know who took it, but you don't want to believe it."

Everyone was waiting, but there was nothing else she could tell the woman, so she went back up on the stage, where the master of ceremonies took over again. He asked her a lot of questions about how long she had been able to see these things and how often she was wrong.

Angie looked at him thoughtfully. "Sometimes I don't want to know something, so I don't think about it. But sometimes I want something to happen so much that I tell myself it *will* happen." She broke off and shrugged. "Like getting a kitten. I keep believing that when we move I can have a pet of my very own, but Grandmother hates cats and they make Celia sneeze."

He asked her about her grandmother and Celia, and then asked if they were with her. Angie said no, but her mother was sitting in the front row. The camera obligingly swung to pick up her mother.

A young fellow in the audience asked if Angie could tell what he was holding and she grinned.

"Yes, you're holding your girl's hand. Her hand has a ring on it."

There was a lot of laughter and applause as the girl next to the young man squealed and held up her hand.

Angie was glad when another act was introduced, and she could sit back and relax. But when the show was over and the lights on all the cameras had blinked off for the last time, she was surrounded by people fussing over her. Her mother came up from the audience, and Miss Crewe was there trying to get them away to the dressing rooms. "Honey, you'll have to get some of that stuff washed off your face. If you go out in the sunlight, it will harden into a mask."

Angie followed obediently and washed her face. She brushed her hair too, but the stuff they had sprayed on made it feel stiff and untidy.

When she returned to her mother she found out that they were all going to the movie star's apartment for a party.

"You'll like that, won't you, sweetie?" Her mother's eyes were sparkling.

No one but Angie noticed the hippy-looking fellow in the dark suit who hovered in the background. When he caught her eye he made an approving circle with his thumb and forefinger, and then gave her a little bow. She wanted to laugh, but she didn't, and when she turned away to answer someone who had spoken to her, he disappeared.

Maybe he'll be at the party, she told herself, as they were climbing into taxis, and at the same moment knew that he wouldn't.

The apartment was huge, just like one in the movies, with shallow stairs going down into the living room and a balcony overhanging the street. Angie was so tired that all she wanted to do was go back to the hotel and sleep, but there were people milling around, smiling at her and patting her, making a fuss over her. She couldn't seem to stop yawning, and finally her hostess took Angie by the hand and led her up a stairway and into a bedroom.

"Okay, youngster, you've had it. Slip off your shoes, and we'll hang your dress over this chair. No sense in mussing the pretty dress." As she spoke she was turning down the bed, plumping the pillow, and helping Angie off with her dress. "Okay, sweetie, just hop in and conk out. I'll tell your mother where you are so she won't worry. It really would be a shame to make her leave the party. She's having *such* a good time."

Angie nodded, slipped off her shoes, and crept gratefully between the cool sheets. There was an elegant gold statue standing on the dressing table. "Is that an Oscar?" she asked sleepily.

"Yes, honey. That's an Oscar." The pretty woman pulled the curtains and smiled at Angie from the doorway. "Have a good sleep now."

When she awakened, what seemed like hours and hours later, she was hungry. The noise from the other room had quieted down. Angie strained her ears as she put on her shoes and went into the bathroom to wash her face. Everything was so beautiful she hated to touch anything. The guest towels said *Yours* instead of *His* and *Hers*. There was an assortment of small combs in a plastic box, so Angie took one and tried to make her hair look tidy.

When she went out into the living room, her hostesss saw her at once and came to meet her. "Hi, Angie. Have a nice sleep?"

"Oh yes, thank you very much," Angie said.

The woman dropped her arm across Angie's shoulders and led her to a group in a corner. Her mother was there, looking flushed and excited, with a funny man Angie had seen on television and a quiet woman, who turned out to be the funny man's wife.

But the person who claimed Angie's instant attention was a dark man wearing a plain dark suit and a turban. She knew the headdress was a turban, because she'd seen one in a book at school.

He held out his hands to Angie gravely, not as if he wanted to shake hands but palms up, and without hesitation Angie put both her hands into his.

The chatter and the laughter in that corner of the room died away as they looked at one another.

"Yes," the man said at last. "This is the child."

She could see that he was quite old, older than forty or even fifty, and that his dark eyes were looking into her heart and finding out everything about her. She wanted to pull her hands free, but at the same time she wanted to be quiet and let the peace and warmth and waiting go on for a long, long while.

"This is Doctor Amir Kandesh Akbar," her hostess said, sounding each syllable carefully. "He was supposed to catch a plane, but he didn't want to leave without meeting you. Aren't you flattered, Angie?"

Angie smiled at her new friend. "I'm glad you stayed," she said simply.

He got up and released Angie's hands. "Come," he said. "We will talk."

She followed him to a comfortable sofa across the room, but when he sat down she didn't sit beside him. Instead she sat down on the floor at his feet and looked up at him.

"It is not easy," he said. "It is not easy even when you are old, as I am old. But to be a child, a beautiful child." He put his hand on her head briefly, and then smiled up at Angie's mother, who followed them. "A great gift such as this child has been given must always carry a great responsibility. She is too young to understand, but you are not too young." The way he spoke was more a question than a statement of fact. Angie's mother said nothing.

Doctor Akbar looked back at Angie. "There are many things to guard against." He leaned forward and took one of Angie's hands, held it palm up for a moment studying the lines, and then, without releasing the hand, he went on talking. "There is a man very close to you, Angie. Not your father.

"My father left us," Angie said. "He went away before Stacy died."

"You loved your father very much. You will always be looking for someone to take his place, not in your life but in your heart. That is because you have a great capacity for loving."

89

Some other people came over to stand around and watch and listen, but Doctor Akbar ignored them. "To be able to see beyond the curtains of time, into the past as well as into the future. . . There are dangers here, Angie, for all of us. It is so easy to tell people what they want to hear, so easy to believe that we *know* when we only hope that something is true." He dropped her hand abruptly. "Do you know what I am trying to say to you, Angie?"

"That I should always tell the truth," Angie said promptly. "That if I don't know I should just *say* I don't know."

A gray-haired man who had been listening leaned forward. "Tell her about the dangers of transference, Doctor," he said in a slightly slurred voice.

"Oh, yes," a woman cooed. "I heard you talk about that one night, Doctor Akbar, and it was just thrilling." She turned to a man beside her. "I don't understand, but it seems that these Indians can *do* it. Just leave their bodies lying around and take their spirit somewhere else. He was telling us about this woman who was seen in Switzerland. She appeared at the side of her dying father and comforted him in his last hours, and all the time her body was lying in a sort of trance back home. . . ."

Someone shushed her, and the woman's voice trailed off uncertainly.

"Is such a thing really possible?" a man asked reasonably. "I mean, you're among friends here, and we aren't going to say anything. . . ."

Doctor Akbar put his hand softly on Angie's head, and she knew the gesture meant good-bye.

She was sorry because having someone who understood, someone who *really* understood, close by, was a comfort.

Jeff met them at the plane and took them to see an apartment in New York City he had found for them.

"Honey," he told her mother earnestly, "you can't live in that run-down suburb now that Angie is going to be a personality. You need a decent address and some good clothes and a chance to enjoy life. Just look at the place, okay?"

They looked at the apartment, which seemed bare and echoing, but there were carpets on all the floors, and the living-room windows looked out on a view of the skyline. Angie's mother loved it, but warned Jeff that her mother would have a fit.

"No, she won't," he said surprisingly. "Your mother has stopped fighting me, haven't you noticed?"

Jeff's claim was true. When Angie stopped and thought about it, she knew it was true. But if Grandmother had stopped fighting Jeff, the change didn't mean that she thought he was right; it meant that she was getting old and tired.

"You wouldn't believe the things we have lined up," Jeff told them, as they drove toward home. "But, of course, we're going to be very choosey. There is a feature article for one of the big weeklies. I got that sewed up just this morning. They wanted to send their own man to do the story and get the pictures, but I told them no dice. I haven't been a journalist all these years for nothing. And another exciting thing. . . The word got out that

91

I've been handling Angie's business, and an old-time star who is trying to get his feet in the TV door called and wanted me to take him on as a client. . . ."

Jeff talked and talked, but he never said a word about being in the audience when Angie was doing her act.

Angie's mother told him all about the studio and the movie star and her glamorous apartment. She forgot to mention meeting Doctor Amir Kandesh Akbar, though. Maybe she didn't think he was very important.

Angie was wedged into the front seat between them letting the talk swirl over and around her.

Jeff slanted a quick grin at her. "Tired, honey?"

"No," she yawned, dropping her cheek against the sleeve of his jacket and falling promptly asleep.

SEVEN

From that time on Angie's life followed much the same pattern. There was a steady stream of TV shows and personal appearances. She met dozens of famous or near-famous celebrities, who were fascinated by her strange gift and perfectly willing to impose on her talent. The family moved to an even more luxurious apartment.

Now Angie was almost fifteen with still another show to do. Rousing herself from the long reverie, she was ready for the onstage call when it came, and the performance went well. Even Jeff was satisfied, despite his concern over her withdrawn mood.

The party for her fifteenth birthday never materialized, because Angie had to go to Los Angeles suddenly for an important benefit.

"But don't be disappointed, sugar. I'll take you to Disneyland, and we'll spend the whole day. How about that?"

She didn't believe they would have time for a private excursion, but she pretended to be pleased. "That will be fun, Jeff. Will Mother and Celia be coming too?"

Jeff gnawed his lip. "We'll only be there a few days, honey. I thought maybe you and me and Laura this time. . ."

They flew to Los Angeles the night before Angie's birthday. Her mother gave her a gorgeous tooled-leather album filled with Angie's clippings so that she could look at it on the plane. Angie knew she'd rather die than open the scrapbook on the plane, but she didn't want to hurt her mother's feelings so she kissed her and thanked her.

Celia gave her some underthings, and her grandmother gave her a book of poetry. Grandmother didn't care for the type of poetry Angie enjoyed and was trying to reeducate her. She wasn't very subtle.

"I think it's just terrible," her mother was still lamenting, when she drove them to the airport. "But never mind, honey. When you get back, we'll celebrate all over again."

"It doesn't matter," Angie said. "I'll have a lot of birthdays, and when would I ever have another chance to meet the Vice President?"

Jeff, who was sitting up front with her mother, turned his head to smile at Angie. "Honey, you'll see the day when the President is trying to get an interview with you."

They stopped and picked up Laura at her apartment. She was packed and ready for them, clearly delighted at the prospect of an unexpected week in Los Angeles. "I was born in Pasadena," she confided to Angie's mother, as they wove through the traffic on the way to the airport. "I have a batch of aunts and cousins scattered around the Los Angeles area."

"I don't especially care for L.A.," Angie's mother said. "All that smog."

For no reason at all Angie found herself remembering the first time they had flown out to California. Then her mother had been wildly excited about the pink shower in the hotel room and the telephone brought to their breakfast table in the dining room. That trip seemed a long time ago, and yet it was only four years back.

"What's the matter, honey?" Jeff asked. "You look sort of sad."

She smiled. "I was thinking about the first time Mother and I flew to California. You wouldn't go along, but we had a marvelous time, didn't we Mother?"

Her mother nodded. "We really did, honey. I didn't think you remembered."

Angie was glad her mother was pleased. She pretended not to notice that Jeff was regarding her narrowly.

When they were on the plane and buckled in for takeoff, Jeff came over and slid into the seat beside her. The stewardess started to object, but Jeff's grin stopped her. "I'm nervous," he said gravely. "Somehow it never seems so scary when I sit by my mother and she holds my hand."

The young woman grinned and moved on down

the aisle, checking seat belts, and asking people to pull their seats upright, please. . . .

"Now what was that all about, Angie?" he asked quietly.

She smiled at him, a carefully bright smile. "What was what all about?" she asked innocently.

Jeff didn't smile. "You wanted your mother and Celia to come along on this trip? Is that it?" When she didn't reply, he went on in the same quiet tone. "Honey, I'm sorry about your birthday, but I'll make it up to you. And if you really wanted the family to come, you only had to say so. . . ."

"I know," she said. "It's just . . . even that first time you didn't want to go with Mother. You were in the audience the next day, and she never even *knew*, because you wore that stupid moustache and a beard."

"The man of many faces," he said lightly. "Jeff, the master sleuth. It was our secret. You never did tell her, did you?"

"No." She turned away from him and looked out the window. "I guess I never told her, because I knew she wouldn't understand. I knew she'd be hurt."

"But you understood."

She nodded, not looking at him. "I understand better now that I'm older, but I understood then, too, a little."

"I didn't want complications, Angie. You probably haven't noticed, but your mother is a very attractive young woman. I thought if I kept out of the way she'd find someone else. . . ."

"But she hasn't." Angie put her head back against the seat and closed her eyes. "She doesn't want to find anyone else, so she never will."

"Look, sugar, she still thinks of herself as married to your father. It's better that way. It keeps the record straight."

"Well, of course, I can see it's better for you," Angie said. "But one of these days Mother is going to notice how much time you spend with Laura. What then?" She opened her eyes and looked at him. "What then, Jeff?"

He didn't answer. He unbuckled his seat belt, went across the aisle, and sat down beside Laura, who immediately put aside her magazine and smiled at him.

Watching them, Angie felt sad and almost old. She wished she knew how Jeff really felt about Laura. Dennis. Sometimes she thought she knew, but she couldn't be sure. A lot of things had happened to change Jeff in the past few years. He didn't work for one paper now; he was a free-lancer and making more money than he ever had dreamed possible. The book that he had been writing all the time Angie was becoming a well-known had appeared at exactly the right time and had become a best seller.

Jeff had set up a trust fund for Angie, and Angie's share of the book royalties went into it. She long since had stopped trying to understand about royalties and annuities and such things. Her mother was always telling people what a good businessman Jeff was.

Her mother. . .

Angie looked across the aisle again and stifled a small sigh. She knew that Jeff wouldn't make the break and marry Laura, however much he wanted to. Only Angie herself would be able to make the decision that would change all their lives, and she wasn't ready . . . not yet . . . perhaps never.

They checked in at the hotel just as they had on a dozen different occasions. Laura shared the suite with Angie. Jeff had a room on another floor.

She was really fond of Laura. At first they had a lot of fun together. Somehow this time was different, and Angie wasn't really surprised when after an hour or two and a half a dozen telephone calls Laura announced that she was going out to visit a cousin for a few hours. "You don't mind, do you, Angie? You'll just be going to bed anyway." She was leaning toward the glass applying fresh lipstick as she spoke. "I'll be terribly quiet when I come in so I won't disturb you."

"Aren't you going to wear your wig?" Angie asked, and Laura shook her head.

"Not tonight. My family doesn't think of me as a blonde."

When she had gone, Angie walked to the window and looked down twenty-two stories into the tinselly night. She didn't know whether Laura was going to meet Jeff or not, but if she did Angie hoped they both would have a miserable evening.

It wasn't even ten o'clock, and she didn't feel like watching TV, but she didn't want to go down to the lobby either. Once before she had tried leaving the room by herself, and some girl in the coffee shop had recognized her. She'd signed autographs for half an hour before the head desk clerk was alerted and came to rescue her.

Jeff had warned her never to try any such thing again. If she wanted to go out for a bite to eat, she only had to call him. On an impulse she picked up the phone and asked for Jeff's room. It rang for a long time before the girl cut in to tell her that the party did not answer.

She walked into the bedroom and immediately saw the hatbox that held Laura's blond wig. It was a beautiful and probably very expensive wig.

I'm not stealing it, Angie reminded herself, as she wound her long hair into hit-or-miss pin curls. And I certainly won't hurt it. I'll be back before they are. . . .

The wig made an exciting difference. She looked older and slightly wicked. Sitting down, she put on more makeup: eye shadow, more exotic lipstick, and a dusting of powder. Laura's tweed coat was hanging in the closet. Angie slipped her arms into it and whirled around to examine her reflection in the mirror. Good! She didn't look anything like Angie Scofield. She looked like . . . like Nancy Drew . . . like Jane Doe . . . like . . . like Sharon Trent. Sharon always had been her favorite name. Tonight she would be Sharon Trent.

She slipped her wallet and the hotel key into one of the large pockets. Without a purse, she wouldn't look like a tourist. No one gave her a second glance in the elevator, and when she emerged into the lobby, she allowed herself to be carried along with the crowd toward the dimly lighted passageway at the rear of the hotel.

And then suddenly a pair of very broad shoulders blocked her way. "Sorry, miss. May I see your ID card?"

She blinked. "ID?"

"No minors allowed in the cocktail lounge, or maybe you were going in the wrong direction. The coffee shop is to your left as you pass the elevator."

She made her way back to the main lobby, but

instead of turning into the coffee shop she went outside and stood for a moment looking first in one direction and then another. The doorman tipped his hat. "Taxi, miss?" he asked, and when she nodded he conjured up a cab with one commanding sweep of his arm.

"Where to?" the driver asked, when she was safely in the cab.

Angie batted her eyes at him. "Nowhere, just drive around, please." She leaned back as he put the car into gear and they shot out into the traffic.

The cabbie grinned. "You don't really want to just drive around? How about a movie? Or a bowling alley? Bowling is a nice clean sport for kids."

"All right," Angie said agreeably. "A bowling alley."

He drove her a few blocks, made a right turn, and they were at the bowling alley. She took his word that the building was a bowling alley, although it looked like a department store or glass-fronted supermarket. She paid the driver and stepped into a strange world of noise and bright lights and confusion. No one paid any attention to her. There were lots of kids around, and older people, too.

Angie found a seat and slid into it. This evening was the first time she ever had watched anyone bowling except for a couple of times when there were programs on TV. There were half a dozen young people, about her own age, bowling on the lanes directly in front of her. Three girls and three boys. Once in a while one of them looked back and smiled at Angie.

Another boy joined them after a while. They all

seemed to know one another very well, and there were a great many friendly insults called back and forth. Being part of such a group would be fun. They probably went to the same school, had parents who visited each other, and shared a dozen different enthusiasms. In the normal course of events they even might marry.

She didn't know when she became aware that they were talking about her. The attention didn't bother her. Instead she knew a quiet satisfaction that they were discussing her as a *girl* instead of Angie Scofield, girl mystic. She wasn't surprised when one of the boys detached himself from the group and came back to slide into the seat beside her.

He was a tall skinny boy with a pleasantly homely face. She knew right away that he came from a good family, brushed his teeth regularly, went to church, and probably got along well with everyone. "Hi," he said easily. "You go to Roosevelt High, right?"

She smiled. "Wrong. I don't even live here. I'm a visitor."

He looked only a little nonplused. "Oh? A couple of the guys" — he motioned toward his friends — "were sure they knew you. We've been having an argument about it, as a matter of fact." His eyes still were studying her face. "You aren't just putting me on? You really are a tourist?"

"That's right."

He shook his head. "I could swear I've seen you before." Then he grinned, a quick boyish grin. "Hey now, maybe I've seen you in my dreams!"

She looked at him teasingly. "You're subject to nightmares?"

The boy chuckled, and then suddenly remembered his manners. "My name is Sam. Sam Kelly."

Angie didn't hesitate. "Sharon," she told him. "Sharon Trent." They shook hands properly, and then Sam jerked his head toward the others. "We'd like you to join us if you aren't waiting for another party. The girls usually bowl against the boys. Do you have a pretty good average?"

"A pretty good average what?" Angie asked, and he laughed and pulled her to her feet.

"What size shoe do you wear?" he squinted down at her feet. "Five? Five and a half?"

"Thanks loads. I take a seven."

"Okay, seven!"

He turned and started toward the desk. Angie followed, feeling amused and disappointed at the same time. "No, please, Sam. You don't understand. I don't even *play*."

He looked at her blankly. "Play? You mean you don't *bowl*?"

"Yes, that's exactly what I mean."

"C'mon!" his grin was disbelieving. "It doesn't matter if you have a low average. The gals can use your handicap." Something in her face finally convinced him she wasn't being coy.

He hesitated a moment before he said, "Would you like to learn, Sharon? You don't have to be a marvel to throw a ball down an alley."

"I'd like to try," she said. "It doesn't look too difficult."

Sam rented a pair of shoes for her and showed her how to find a ball to fit her hand. They walked back to join his friends, and Sam made hurried introductions. Pat, Marcia, Phil, Sally . . . The names and faces didn't fit, but Angie smiled and nodded and murmured "Hello."

She found that bowling wasn't as easy at it looked. The ball was heavy, and she felt awkward and self-conscious going up to the line. Sam was patient and encouraging, however. He told her everyone threw gutter balls occasionally, and by the time they had bowled the first line Angie was beginning to feel a little more confident.

"At least, we'll have your handicap, Sharon," one of the girls assured her. "We always bowl handicap when we take on these monsters."

Angie sat next to Sam and tried to figure out how he was keeping score. It looked terribly complicated. Once she got lucky and knocked down all the pins with the first ball.

"Strike!" Marcia yelled happily.

Angie felt as though she had found herself in a strange country, rubbing elbows with the natives and trying to understand what they were talking about.

One of the boys collected dimes and went to get Cokes for everyone. Angie opened her wallet and gave him a dollar bill, explaining apologetically that she was out of change. When he returned with the Cokes he counted out her change carefully.

"We always go Dutch treat," one of the girls explained. "I don't know how they do it at your school." There was a faint question behind the words.

103

"I go to an all-girls school," Angie found herself replying. "Everything is Dutch."

They were all so friendly and had accepted her so readily that Angie found herself thinking. This is what I would have been doing if I were just plain Angie Scofield. This is what I've missed.

The girl called Sally gave her some pointers about the way Angie was throwing her ball. "You're trying too hard," she said. "It's better if you just roll it *gently* as if you were rolling it across the floor to a baby."

Angie thanked her and watched as Sally threw the ball. She noticed that Sally was wearing a ring on her engagement finger. Not a real engagement ring, it looked more like a class ring.

Angie looked around at the boys, trying to decide which one . . . which one. . . . The boy called Phil? Angie looked at him thoughtfully. Someone nudged her. Her turn to bowl had come.

She couldn't believe her ears when one of the girls said it was twelve thirty and she had to be going. They all trooped to the desk together and paid for their bowling. Sally had to borrow thirty-five cents from Phil, because she didn't have quite enough. They parted in a noisy, friendly fashion.

"If you're around next Friday, we'll be seeing you," Sally called across her shoulder.

Finally they all had gone except Sam, and he was regarding her uneasily, as if he didn't know exactly what to do about her. "I wish I could offer to take you home, Sharon, but I don't have a car."

"Don't worry about it," Angie said. "I'll take a cab at the hotel stand I saw down the block."

He looked surprised. "Won't that be expensive?"

A warning bell chimed in her subconscious. She couldn't tell him she was staying at the hotel. "It isn't far. Just too far to walk. I'll catch a cab."

He frowned. "Look, I could call home and ask my brother to come and pick us up."

She shook her head. "No, honestly, a cab will be fine." And then, because he still looked undecided, she added, "I really had fun, Sam, and thanks loads for asking me to bowl."

She slipped her arms into Laura's tweed coat, and Sam followed her outside. Slowly they walked toward the cab stand.

"I'll see you again, won't I?" he asked, and she nodded.

"Oh yes, you'll see me again."

"We usually bowl on Fridays," he said. "If you're still in town, maybe you'll drop around."

"Maybe I will," she said, knowing that she wouldn't.

The cab shot off on a call just as they reached the stand, and its disappearance was almost like a reprieve. "If I had your telephone number I could call you," Sam said, but she shook her head.

"No, I really couldn't. This . . . aunt I'm visiting is pretty stuffy about things." She wasn't a good liar, and she could see he didn't believe her, so she improvised swiftly. "I'll call *you*, Sam. If I can't make it to the bowling alley next Friday, I'll call you there. Okay?"

A cab pulled up and the driver merely glanced at them. A couple of teenage kids probably didn't seem like a very likely fare.

"Tell me about Sally and Phil," Angie said. "I noticed she's wearing a ring."

Sam grinned. "Sally's engaged, but not to Phil. Some guy who lives in Boston, I think. Anyway, Sally still runs around with the old gang."

"But she's going to marry Phil. Just as soon as they're out of school. And they'll live happily ever after." She turned from his astonished face and got into the cab. "Good-bye, Sam. Be seeing you."

The cab driver looked back to her. "Where to, miss?"

"The Bay Towers," she said, hoping that Sam didn't hear. She lifted her hand in farewell as the cab whirled out into the traffic.

EIGHT

The first thing she saw when the cab drew up before the hotel entrance was Jeff. He was talking excitedly to the doorman, and a policeman was standing nearby, listening but contributing nothing to the conversation. All three men turned and stared as Angie got out of the cab and calmly paid the driver.

Jeff's face was such a study of anger and relief that Angie wanted to smile, but she kept her face and her voice carefully expressionless. "Hi, Jeff. What's the excitement?"

She hadn't noticed the man lounging in the doorway until the flash bulb exploded. Automatically she turned away from the flash, and at once Jeff was at her side, grasping her arm and steering her expertly through the people in the lobby. He shepherded her into the elevator and punched the button for the right floor without saying a single word.

Laura evidently heard them coming, for she was waiting in the doorway, and Angie noticed at once that she'd been crying.

When the door closed behind them, Jeff released his hold on her arm. She was prepared for his being annoyed. She was even resigned to the fact that Laura would probably lecture her in her mild, just-between-us-girls fashion. What she hadn't expected was Jeff's very real anger, his all-out-of-proportion anger.

"Would it be too much to ask what the hell is going on?" he asked with a deceptive mildness that was more frightening than a roar. "You do know how to write, don't you? You could have left a note."

"I didn't think of it," Angie said stiffly. "Anyway, I didn't have any plans. I just wanted to go somewhere. I'm sorry if you were worried."

"Now why would we be worried? A fourteen-year-old girl simply walks out of a Los Angeles hotel and disappears. . . ."

"Fifteen," Angie said. "I'm fifteen, and I said I was sorry if you were worried. I called your room and you were out, and so was Laura. So I got dressed up and went to a bowling alley to watch some kids bowl."

"Take off that stupid wig," Jeff said. "You look like a cheap chorus girl"

Angie didn't have any idea what a chorus girl looked like, but she was sure the observation wasn't complimentary. If Laura resented the remark about her blond wig, she managed to hide her feelings.

"I didn't hurt the wig," Angie said. "I just wore it so I wouldn't be recognized."

"Fine," Jeff said. "I'm sure the reporter and the photographer who got that shot of you leaving the cab had no idea that under that blond haystack was the real Angie Scofield."

"I've said I'm sorry," she reminded him. "How was I supposed to know you'd be raising a hue and cry? I didn't think you and Laura would be back for hours. I didn't even think you'd miss me."

"I've asked you not to go off by yourself. We had a gentleman's agreement about that, when you almost were mobbed in the coffee shop."

Angie took off the wig and replaced it carefully on its Styrofoam head. "How did the reporter find out I was gone? You didn't call the newspaper . . . ?"

"Of course not, I called the police. The reporter was probably hanging around waiting for a story to happen. I called the hotel half a dozen times before I got worried and came back. No one had seen you. The girl at the desk said there had been no phone calls and no visitors. . . ." Jeff paused and lighted a cigarette. He probably didn't realize that his hands were unsteady. "Even the doorman couldn't remember."

"He saw me; he even called a cab. He just didn't recognize the new me."

Jeff looked at her. "Don't quibble, Angie. This isn't a big joke."

Angie looked from Jeff to Laura, who hadn't

contributed a syllable to the discussion, and then back to Jeff. "I know it isn't a big joke," she said softly. "But I can't help wondering whether all this concern is because you thought I was lost or because you wouldn't have anyone to appear at the benefit tomorrow."

He looked as if she had hit him, and Angie was sorry almost before the words were uttered, but some streak of cruelty she hadn't known she possessed made her go on. "Well, of course, I realize how embarrassing it would be for you to admit that your trained seal had escaped while you were out living it up. Explaining to my mother and grandmother would be particularly difficult."

Jeff's eyes were stunned. He was looking at her as if she were a complete stranger.

"Angie, dear," Laura started to say, but Jeff merely glanced at her and she fell silent.

In the quiet Jeff walked over to the window and stared down into the swirling traffic and kaleidoscope of lights. He spoke without turning his head. "Is that what you really believe, Angie? That I don't care anything about you?"

She wanted to cry, but she wanted to hurt him, too. The sensation was almost as if she were standing outside herself watching another Angie Scofield snap the whip that could make Jeff flinch.

"But, of course, you care about me," she said. "I am a — what was it the man said — a very valuable property. You've invested a lot of time and money in me, and you don't want to have it all go down the drain." She didn't look at him; if she did all the brittle coldness would dissolve. She knew Jeff loved her, he couldn't love her any more

110

if he were her own father, but he wasn't her own father.

"I'm sorry if you believe that, Angie," he said, and his voice wasn't anything like Jeff's voice.

As if on cue the telephone rang, and Jeff walked over to pick up the receiver.

Angie and Laura listened as he explained, patiently at first, that there was really no story, that it was just a misunderstanding, a message that hadn't been delivered. The police call . . . yes, he had called the police, but it was a mistake. The man on the other end of the line kept talking, and Jeff tried to be civil, but finally he gave up, said good night firmly, and hung up.

Almost at once the phone rang again. This time it was the policeman who was still waiting in the lobby.

"I'll be right down," Jeff said. He waited a few seconds, then dialed the desk, and asked that no more calls be put through. "That's right. Ask them to leave a name and number, and if the call is important I'll return it. Thank you. Yes, I'd appreciate that."

He put down the phone carefully and walked to the door. "You won't be bothered by any more calls, but it might be a good idea if you get some sleep. Good night, Laura. Good night, Angie."

The door closed behind him, and she was alone with Laura, who looked as if she might be ready to cry again.

She didn't really care about trying to hurt Laura. Laura wasn't that important. "I'm tired," Angie said bleakly. "I think I'll go to bed."

"That sounds like a good idea," Laura said a

little too heartily. "Tomorrow will be a big day."

They talked very little afterward. Normally Laura was an effervescent companion, but tonight the sparkle was missing. Clearly Laura had something on her mind. If she *had* been with Jeff when Angie turned up missing, what would be more natural than that Jeff had blamed her? Well, maybe not blamed her, but held her jointly responsible.

In the darkness she turned her head and looked across toward the other twin bed. "I'm sorry about borrowing your wig," she said, "and I'm sorry about spoiling your evening."

Laura spoke quickly, "I don't mind about the wig, Angie, and you didn't really spoil my evening. It was just that Jeff got so upset, and then when we got back to the hotel and you were still missing . . ." Her voice dwindled off, as if she realized that she was betraying herself.

Angie punched her pillow and turned her head tiredly. "Anyway it doesn't matter, does it? The strayed lamb returned. . . ."

She closed her eyes determinedly and thought about the earlier events of the evening, trying to bring back the warm feeling of being young and just like everybody else, trying to pull Sam's pleasant grin from the well of her memory. She half smiled, remembering the way he had sauntered up to her at the bowling alley. The thought hadn't occurred to him that she might snub him, because she looked familiar. They all believed she went to — what was the name of the school? — oh yes, Roosevelt High.

Telling Jeff and Laura about the evening would

have been fun. Jeff was always bemoaning the fact that Angie didn't have what he called a "normal adolescenthood."

There was her school, for example. She didn't go to a regular school like Celia's, but to a special school for professionals. Most of her classmates were in the theatre or making movies or working in a TV series. A couple of girls did nothing but commercials. There were only seven boys in the entire school, and they paid absolutely no attention to Angie. No one thought of Angie as peculiar, because everyone was different. Some of the girls were on friendly terms, although the feeling that they were all in competition discouraged any intimate friendships. Miss Conover, who was head of the school, made a great to-do about holiday parties and twice-a-year dances. She said her girls shouldn't miss out on the fun part of being high-school students, but the effort was forced and none of the girls were very interested. They all had full and busy lives away from school, and most of them had as much social life as they could handle. As one of the girls had remarked to Angie when she first enrolled, "You won't get any rah-rah team spirit at Conover's, but you'll learn how to read and spell and write thank-you notes."

Celia thought going to Miss Conover's would be the absolute end, but she couldn't go because the classes were limited to professional children. As a matter of fact, Celia made no secret of the fact that she envied Angie. Sometimes Angie had the distinct feeling that Celia more than resented her. But when she tried to explain this situation to her grandmother, she was horrified.

"What do you mean, Celia hates you? Of course, she doesn't hate you. She's your sister!"

There was no point in arguing the matter. Grandmother's beliefs fitted into neat little molds. She was much happier feeling that Angie and Celia loved one another because they were sisters.

Angie turned her pillow again. She hoped that the reporters wouldn't descend on her in the morning. At first she had enjoyed the interviews, but just as first . . .

Once during the first hectic year of her rise to prominence, she was being interviewed and a woman had asked Angie how she got herself in the mood for her act. Did she have to make her mind a complete blank and wait for her subconscious to take over?

Angie thought about the question seriously for a moment, not quite sure how to explain.

"It's better when I don't have to think about the questions. The answers just come out and I never know — well, I hardly ever know — when I've been right or wrong. Because people *remember* when you tell them something that's true."

"You mean if you told me I was going to meet a tall handsome dark stranger and marry him, and then I married a short blond man I'd just remember that you'd told me I was going to get married. Right?"

Angie smiled, a small secretive smile. "I wouldn't tell you anything like that. Because you *are* married. . . ."

The woman looked startled for a second; then she leaned forward toward Angie. "How did you do that, Angie? Assuming that no one told you I was married. How did you know?"

"When you were talking just now about the tall handsome stranger and the short blond man, I could see you with a man who was your husband."

"What do you mean you could *see* . . . ?"

"It was more as if I could *remember*," Angie said slowly. "The way you pass someone on the street, and you hardly look at him, but afterward you can remember what he looks like. He has a nice smile, and he wears glasses, and . . ." She hesitated.

"And what? Anyone could have a nice smile and wear glasses, Angie."

"He limps," Angie said. "Not much, just a little. When he walks, he holds one shoulder higher than the other, so people won't notice."

The woman nodded. "Okay, honey, I'm sold." She closed her notebook with a snap and got to her feet. "Excuse me, Angie. I am about to go out and meet a tall man with a sweet smile, glasses, and a limp. And whether he knows it or not he's going to buy me a big fat martini. I feel as if I could use one."

She awakened the next morning when she heard Laura moving softly about the room, but she pretended to be asleep until she heard the bathroom door close and water running in the shower. Then she sat up cautiously and looked across the room to where the dressing-table mirror threw back her reflection.

Fifteen, I am fifteen years old, she told herself solemnly. Happy birthday, Angie. Happy, happy birthday . . .

There was a soft tap at the door, the special tap

that Jeff always used. The water was still running in the shower. Angie windmilled her arms into her robe and ran barefoot to the door. She slipped the chain from the safety lock and opened the door, smiling into Jeff's startled eyes.

"Good morning, Jeff. Isn't it a beautiful day?"

"You're supposed to find out who's at the door before you open it," he began automatically, and then smiled and shook his head. "Yes, it *is* a beautiful day. Happy birthday, honey, happy fifteenth birthday."

Angie sighed contentedly. The happiness that had been just a shadow away enveloped her. Saying "I'm sorry" and that she hadn't meant all the things she'd said the night before wouldn't be necessary.

"I brought the papers," Jeff said. "The picture isn't very good, but I thought we'd better know what they have to say before your mother calls."

They spread out the papers, and Angie made a little face when she saw the picture of a young blond girl alighting from a cab. She hadn't even noticed when they took that one. "I look all legs," she said.

The newspaper story wasn't important. It suggested slyly that Angie Scofield's mysterious disappearance might well be a publicity stunt to advertise her appearance on a benefit show that evening. It went on to list the other people who would be on the show, including the Vice President.

Laura came out of the bathroom and looked a little upset to find Jeff there. She hadn't taken time to put on her makeup so she disappeared again almost immediately.

"Shall we have breakfast up here?" Jeff asked. "Or shall we brave the mob in the dining room?"

"Couldn't we go somewhere else?" Angie asked wistfully. "We were always going to take a sightseeing trip. I know we won't have time today, but . . ."

"Who says we won't have time? We have all the time in the world." He lifted his voice. "Hey, Laura, how about breakfast by the ocean?"

Laura came to the doorway, smoothing her eyebrow with a practiced forefinger. "Why don't you and Angie go without me this time? I really do have some telephone calls to make."

Angie had an idea that Laura could be persuaded easily to change her mind, and she almost held her breath until Jeff said that they'd better get going.

"Want to order your breakfast up here?" he asked Laura, but she shook her head.

"Oh no, I'd better skip breakfast. Randy will probably want to take me to lunch."

Neither of them asked who Randy was, so if she was trying to make Jeff jealous, the effort was wasted. He went on reading the paper while Angie dressed, and when the phone rang he reached for it quickly.

As they had expected Angie's mother was calling to find out what had happened: why Angie was reported missing, why she was wearing that terrible blond wig . . .

Jeff soothed her as only Jeff could when she was upset. "Honey, it was just a big fat misunderstanding. We didn't get Angie's message that she was watching this bowling tournament. . . ." He crossed his fingers solemnly and held them up for Angie and Laura to see. "She thought it would be fun to wear the wig, and we hoped that people wouldn't recognize her. . . ." He went on talking, making the incident sound like a big joke, and after a moment he handed the phone to Angie so she could say good morning and have her mother and grandmother wish her a happy birthday.

Celia didn't come to the phone; she was still in bed.

"In bed? Oh sure, this is Saturday. I forgot about that."

Her grandmother reminded her to be careful. Her mother sounded wistful when Angie told her Jeff was taking her out for breakfast.

"Have fun, honey," she said, "but don't get too strung up and come down with another of those headaches. . . ."

Angie hung up the phone regretfully. Just hearing her mother's voice, her grandmother's voice, always made her feel unaccountably young.

Jeff called a cab, and they drove to the ocean and had a marvelous breakfast. There weren't many people in the restaurant that early. No one recognized Angie, or if they did, no one bothered to come to the table to ask for her autograph or to tell her they had seen her on television.

"Last night," she told Jeff, when they were waiting for the waiter to bring their order, "at the bowling alley, some kids asked me if I wanted to bowl with them. They thought they knew me. Do you suppose it was because they might have seen my face when I was doing some show and just didn't connect me with being a blonde?"

118

"Could be," Jeff said. "It's a funny thing about television. Mort and I were talking about it just the other day. When you appear on television you come into a person's home. It's something completely different from being a nightclub entertainer or in a Broadway show. People feel that they know you. That's why people who write to you say 'Dear Angie,' instead of 'Dear Miss Scofield.'"

She nodded, and then went on. "Anyway there was this boy, an awfully nice boy named Sam. He hinted that he'd like to see me again."

"I see," Jeff said, as if he really did see, "and what about you, Angie? Would you like to see him again?"

"I guess so. Only, only if he knew I was *Angie* it might spoil things. I told him my name was Sharon. It was like, like taking a part in a play. Only I didn't know my lines, and I had to ad lib." The waiter had returned noiselessly and served their juice and Jeff's coffee. Jeff didn't like Angie to drink coffee, so she drank milk whenever he was around. At home with her grandmother she drank coffee. Her grandmother said if she was old enough to support an entire family she was certainly old enough to drink coffee.

Angie took a sip of her orange juice. "I wonder if Sam and the other kids will see my picture in the paper and recognize me. Do you suppose they could, Jeff?"

"It's possible," he admitted. "Why, does it bother you that they might?"

"I don't know. It's just that I told Sam if we were still in Los Angeles next week that I might come to the bowling alley and see him. But maybe

119

if he thinks I was lying to them and just giving him a line, he might not want me to come."

Jeff was regarding her carefully. "Why is this boy important, honey? You've always steered so clear of boys up until now. I didn't think you liked boys."

Angie grinned. "They scare me, that's all. I never know what to say to them, and anyway the only boys I ever see are the ones at school, and they aren't like regular boys."

Jeff's eyes twinkled. "I'm sure they'd be fascinated to hear it."

"You know what I mean. The boys at school are kids with *careers*. Do you realize that when Miss Conover forced all of us to attend that dance last Christmas not one single solitary boy asked me to dance? Not that I *cared* especially. . . ."

"Of course, you cared," Jeff said. "Otherwise, you wouldn't even remember it. But one thing is, Angie, that in a few years these same boys will be standing in line to have a dance with you."

"Why?" Angie wasn't fishing for compliments; she really wanted to know. "Why, Jeff?"

"Because you are starting to be a very beautiful girl. There is a kind of glow about you that will attract men like flies, and besides that you are kind, sympathetic, and have a lovely sense of humor." He held out his hand, palm up. "A quarter, please."

Angie opened her handbag and searched until she found a quarter, which she passed to him with a smile.

"Thank you, Jeff. I love to listen to all this stuff even if it isn't true."

"It is truer than you think. I almost wish it

wasn't. Life is going to be tough enough for you. If you are beautiful as well as famous, it could be a disaster."

The waiter came with their breakfast, and Angie ate with huge enjoyment. Once she slanted a quick grin across the table at Jeff. "As long as today is Saturday I don't see why I have to do any schoolwork, Jeff. Laura is so fussy about my assignments, but since today is my birthday . . ."

Jeff shrugged. "Honey, you know I don't get into that routine. You'll have to try your wiles on Laura. After all, it's her job and her responsibility to see that you are properly educated."

They didn't get back to the hotel until almost noon. Jeff had some business to take care of, so he left Angie at the elevator. Laura was just getting ready to go out. She had some assignments for Angie, but agreed that Angie might skip them.

."Did you and Jeff have fun?" she asked.

Angie said, "Yes, lots of fun."

"There were some calls for you," Laura went on, squinting into the dressing-table mirror to see if her eyelashes were applied properly. "I guess there must be a new girl on the switchboard. She didn't know anything about Jeff putting a hold on the calls."

"Oh," Angie said. "Was it anyone special?"

"Someone named Sam. Do you know anyone in Los Angeles, Angie? I didn't realize you'd been here before."

"Did he leave a number?" Angie asked.

"No, he seemed in a hurry. Said he'd call back." Laura was apparently satisfied with her eyelashes at last. She whirled away from the mirror and went to pick up her coat. "Maybe you'd better take a rest this afternoon, Angie. The benefit doesn't start until eight, but we're supposed to be there at six thirty. Something about new lighting they want to try."

When she was alone Angie sat and stared at the telephone, willing Sam to call back, but knowing at the same time that he wouldn't. It was Saturday. He was probably with his gang somewhere, or maybe he had a weekend job. Anyway whatever had prompted him to call, she was depressingly sure that he wouldn't call again.

But the mere fact that he had called and asked for Angie meant that he had seen the newspaper story and had recognized her from the picture. Somehow that spoiled things. Last night she had been a girl named Sharon. Sharon might have gone back to the bowling alley on Friday and met Sam again. But Angie couldn't. Could she?

NINE

Angie tried to take a nap as the afternoon dragged on, but she couldn't fall asleep. She tried reading, but couldn't seem to concentrate. There were no more telephone calls. Angie turned on the TV. When nothing interesting came on, she turned it off again.

Her hands were beginning to feel clammy, and she was aware of a warning pulse that beat in her throat. Maybe I'm going to get sick; maybe I've got that flu that's been going around. To be safe, she took a couple of aspirin, aware, even as she did so, that they were merely a gesture. Her grandmother was a firm believer in aspirin. "You look a little peaked, better take a couple of aspirin." She almost could hear her grandmother saying the words. For years Angie had thought that looking "peaked" meant that her head was coming to a point. When she was very small, she used to rub the top of her head worriedly.

Angie paced from one end of the room to the other. *Something is going to happen. Something is going to happen.* She sat down and waited for the feeling to go away, but it persisted.

When Jeff tapped softly at the door, she crossed the room with effort and let him in. Being Jeff, he sensed instantly that something was bothering her. "What's the matter, honey? Something wrong?"

She shook her head, and then managed to give him a quick smile. "I don't know. I just have this . . . this *waiting* feeling. Something is going to happen. I don't even know what it is." She shook her head again, as if to clear away the notion.

Jeff smiled at her easily, but she could see that his eyes were concerned. "Maybe you're getting stage fright. That's quite a production they've planned for tonight. You should see the dressing rooms, the last word, And the theatre is crawling with security guards for the Vice President. No one will be admitted without a ticket and the proper identification."

Angie listened without really hearing what he was saying.

Laura came in after a while, and Jeff ordered tea and sandwiches sent up to the room. Angie didn't feel hungry, but Jeff pointed out that they wouldn't be able to eat again for hours. You couldn't tell about these benefit affairs; sometimes they dragged on forever.

Laura chattered on brightly about her day, and Jeff told them about the new singing group he had interviewed. "I know that folk groups are on the way out, but these kids really have something. I think they'll probably make it big."

"How young?" Laura asked. "Don't forget, if you get a young group you run into all sorts of hassles about having them appear in places where drinks are served. . . ."

Angie listened without adding anything to the conversation. She had the feeling that she had lived through this identical scene in another time, another place. She knew to the word what Laura was going to say, what Jeff would answer. She felt as if she were watching an old play and had memorized all the lines.

The sensation was something that happened more and more frequently, usually when she was with people she knew very well, but occasionally with strangers, too. Like the man at the university who had wanted her to take those tests. . . .

Jeff looked at her suddenly. "You're smiling," he said. "I hope that means you're feeling better."

"I'm fine," she said, not quite truthfully.

Angie was used to appearances now, and the tension before a performance never bothered her. Still, a headache that was probably the result of her anxiety earlier in the day began to come on, so she took another aspirin and then a tranquilizer. The show was late getting started, but the audience didn't seem to mind. Angie could feel the excitement. Having uniformed security guards all over the place gave the affair an all-out-of-proportion importance.

When she was introduced and had acknowledged the applause she took her place, lifting her cheek to the master of ceremonies so that he could kiss her. Why did everyone kiss everybody? People didn't mean anything by the gesture, not really. She met the Vice President, shaking hands with him when they were introduced. At least he didn't kiss her. She felt the pressure of his strong fingers and knew that he was a wise and just man, who would do his best for his country.

"Well, Angie," he said in the voice that was now familiar to millions of Americans. "Have you a message for me?"

His eyes were warm, but Angie could see that they didn't really believe her. She held on to his hand with both of hers. "You will be a good president," she said clearly, "but I won't be able to vote for you the first time. I won't be old enough."

There was a ripple of nervous laughter and then silence. The big man looked at her seriously. "Is this a prophecy, my dear?"

She smiled at him. "It's just what we both know," she said.

The master of ceremonies came forward and led the Vice President to his chair. Angie sat very still looking out at the audience and trying to identify the little feathering of fear that brushed her consciousness.

Father! She could feel his presence so clearly that the sensation was like a stab of electricity. Her father was out there! She almost got to her feet, but remembered in time where she was, remembered that three television cameras were following her every movement.

When the moment came for her performance, she was sure that she wouldn't be able to do anything. She felt drained and saddened. The tranquilizer probably was doing its work too well. Since that long-ago appearance when she had moved through the audience touching people's hands as she tried to answer their questions, the procedure had remained standard. Audiences like it. She looked into a woman's face and listened to her voice asking something about some stocks and bonds. She touched the woman's arm gently. "I'm sorry. There are no stocks and bonds. You may as well stop looking. But stocks and bonds wouldn't make you happy. What *will* make you happy. . . ." She paused and bit her lip thoughtfully. "There is someone standing close to you, holding out his hand in friendship. He works at a desk. You work in the same place. You smile at him, but don't really see him. You should look more closely."

The woman sat down abruptly. She didn't even say thank you.

A pretty girl wanted to know if she would be married soon. Angie held her hand for a moment, and then released it slowly. "No," she said. "Not soon. You will have a very glamorous career. The door has not opened yet, but it will soon."

Afterward Angie wasn't sure whether she was really seeing these things or whether they had become a reflex. She moved farther up the aisle, and her eyes swept from side to side, looking for her father. He had to be there, he had to. The feeling was so strong, so sure, that she couldn't escape it.

There was another question, another face swimming before her, and another answer dragged from her subconscious.

"I'm so tired," she told the man with the microphone. "I'm so terribly tired."

His eyes filled with quick concern, and he gestured to a man on stage. Angie started down the aisle, keeping her face carefully emotionless as people reached out to touch her.

The headache was back, pounding at her temples, making a roaring in her ears. Sitting quietly in her chair took effort. The master of ceremonies turned to say something, and she had just a glimpse of the surprise on his face before his features started to swim together. Angie tried to stand up because her chair was rocking from side to side, but she couldn't stand because everything was slipping and sliding away — the other performers and the cameras and the bright lights — everything slipping and sliding into a great vacuum that yawned under her feet.

She clutched the side of her chair and heard a voice calling from a long way off. Her own voice, calling and calling. . . . Father? Father? Where are you? Come back!

She pulled herself out of the clutching fingers of darkness, and the first thing she saw was Jeff's worried face. She was lying on a lounge in one of the dressing rooms, and someone was holding her wrist — not Jeff — a shadowy figure whose face was turned away from her but whose voice was firm and clear. "Now she's coming around. Can you do something about getting this mob out of here? It's like Friday night at the circus."

There was a damp cloth on Angie's forehead and a sharp feeling in her throat and chest, as though she had been inhaling ammonia. She was aware of all the people in the background, curious faces, mouths shaped into questions, and watchful eyes. There was a whispering buzz, just a few disjointed phrases made any sense. "What an exit, feet first!" "Do you suppose she really . . ." "Anything for public . . ."

Someone was trying to shoo the crowd away. And then a firm voice broke through the hubbub. "Clear a path, please. The ambulance is here."

Angie reached for Jeff's hand. "No," she said. "I'm all right. It was just the heat and the lights and everything. Please, Jeff, I don't want to go to the hospital. I'm fine."

The doctor straightened up and shrugged. "She could be right. It probably was just a faint. Her pulse is steady, and her color's come back."

Angie sat up and pushed the cloth away from her forehead. "Jeff, I'm so sorry. Was it awful?"

"Frightening," he admitted, and went to talk to the man who was waiting to hear whether they needed the ambulance.

At last they went back to the hotel in a cab. Angie protested that she felt well enough to stay for the rest of the benefit, but Jeff was firm. "You're booked for a guest shot on one of the women's talk shows Monday morning, and on Tuesday that university professor wants you to do an interview for some paper he's writing on ESP. That's a heavy schedule ahead of you."

Not until they were back in the hotel room and Laura was fussing around treating Angie like a convalescent did Jeff ask, "What spooked you tonight, Angie? I could see there was something wrong."

"I had this feeling that my father was in the audience. He *was* there, Jeff. I could feel it."

Jeff shook his head. "Afraid not, honey. This was a hand-picked crowd, remember. Security guards, admittance passes, the whole bit. If it had been at any of your other performances, I'd say it was highly probable, but not this one. Not unless he works on a paper or magazine or has some important government job. Matter of fact, I had to pull a few coattails to get a pass for Laura, didn't I, honey?"

Angie pretended not to notice the small endearment. "No, he had to be there, Jeff. Unless all this is a lie. Unless I really can't do all these things. Unless the things I see aren't visions and predictions at all, but just an overactive imagination."

Laura had turned from the TV set and was looking at Jeff. "That man," she said, "you know the one who tried to get in without a pass. Didn't he have some story about delivering a message to one of the performers?"

Jeff turned to her sharply. "This is the first I've heard of it."

"It might not be true," Laura said hastily. "I mean, I just heard these people whispering about it."

"Easy enough to check, I suppose." Jeff went at once to the phone, and after a couple of calls he was connected with some person at the studio. The man told Jeff he'd investigate and call him right back.

Jeff turned to Angie with a smile that didn't quite mask his uneasiness. "There! Paul will find out if there's anything to this business. But honey" — he came over and sat down on the arm of a big chair next to her — "if it was your father, if your father knew you were here and wanted to see you, wouldn't he come to the hotel and ask for you? The story was in the papers this morning. He could look you up easily enough."

"Maybe he just wanted to see me," Angie said softly, "just wanted to see me and be sure that I was all right."

He squinted down at her. "Angie, it's been six years. Didn't you ever wonder why he never got in touch with you?"

She shook her head. "No, I never wondered. I tried not to think about him. Sometimes I had the feeling that I could sit down and just . . . you know . . . just concentrate, and I could see him. Where he was, what he was doing."

"Why didn't you then?"

"Because I was afraid," she said honestly. "Afraid he might be dead, but afraid of something else, too. That he might be happy and contented without us. That he might not even think about us very much. . . ."

The telephone rang, and she watched Jeff pick up the receiver and speak into the mouthpiece. He asked a few questions, thanked the man named Paul, and then replaced the telephone.

"It seems there was a man who tried to get in without a pass. Matter of fact, there were four

131

people that the security guards turned away. A couple of them were checked out by the police. No one was held. It's just that with the Vice President there . . ." He stopped and shrugged. "I'm sorry, honey. This doesn't seem to tell us anything."

Angie leaned back in her chair. "He was there," she said. "He came to see me."

All during the rest of that busy week she waited for him to come. When the telephone rang she jumped to answer it. But her father, if her father had come to the benefit, made no further attempt to see her. On Friday evening they were supposed to fly home. Jeff talked to her mother on the phone, but Angie was in the gift shop off the lobby and missed the call.

"Celia is going to be in a play at school," Jeff reported. "She got the leading role. Your mother says she's walking two feet off the ground." There was something else, something he wasn't telling her. Angie wanted to smile, knowing how difficult keeping a secret was for Jeff.

The plane wasn't leaving until midnight. Jeff had a few last-minute things to attend to in town, so they wouldn't be able to make the earlier flight. "Maybe you and Laura would like to see a show," he said.

Laura made a little face and Angie shook her head. "Don't worry about us, Jeff. We'll think of something."

"Where would you like to have dinner, honey?" Laura asked, as the afternoon wore on. "We could call a cab and go to that place by the water that you liked so much. Or there are some fine skyroom restaurants. . . ."

Angie whirled from the window where she had been watching the steady stream of traffic flowing down the avenue and merging into the sweeping arm of a freeway entrance. "Where I would really like to go," she said, "is to the bowling alley. They have a good restaurant — not just hamburgers and that stuff, but food. Only . . ." she paused and dropped her eyes and her voice, sadly, effectively. "Only I don't suppose you'd care for anything like that."

Laura looked nervous. "Honey, you know Jeff wouldn't like us going there. Those young people, they certainly must have seen your picture in the paper and recognized you by now. As a matter of fact, some of them have come to the hotel and asked for your room number. You shouldn't get involved with — "

"When," Angie broke in, "when did they come to see me and why wasn't I *told*? They probably feel awful, being turned away like peddlers or something. They were so nice to me, Laura, as if I were one of them."

"But Angie . . ."

"And I *am* one of them," Angie rushed on. "I bet they'd be glad to see me again. Oh please, Laura. What could happen? You'll be there. If things get sticky, we'll come back to the hotel. *Please?*"

Laura looked undecided, but Angie could see that she was weakening. One of the things that Laura couldn't resist was having Angie treat her as if they were the same age with the same enthusiasms.

"We can go in and have a nice dinner and wait until, oh, around eight thirty or nine. We'll be back an hour before Jeff gets here. Oh, *please*, Laura. Otherwise, I'll never see him again."

"Him?"

"The boy who asked me to bowl with them. Sam. He was such a nice boy."

"Sam? But that's the boy who called, isn't it?"

Angie looked at her sadly. "Yes, but he never called back. What harm could it do to say goodbye?"

They left a note for Jeff, in case he got back before they did. Angie looked up the address and telephone number in the phone book, so he'd know where they were.

"Do you want to wear my wig?" Laura asked, as they were getting ready, but Angie shook her head.

"No, he knows I'm Angie. Otherwise, he wouldn't have known where to call."

They took a cab to the bowling alley before Laura had a chance to change her mind. She looked a little more mollified when she saw that the restaurant was as nice as Angie had promised. They found a booth and studied the menu carefully. Angie made sure she was facing the entrance so she could see the people coming in.

They didn't hurry through the meal, but even so they finished too early. "Now what?" Laura asked, looking across the table at Angie, who was making her pie last as long as possible. "Should we just sit out there and be spectators for a minute?"

"Oh, could we, Laura? That's what I wanted to do."

They found places in almost the exact spot Angie had occupied the week before. Laura watched for a few moments, and then turned her head to smile at Angie. "I used to bowl in a league when I was in school," she said. "Makes me feel a million years old."

"You could find a ball and rent some shoes," Angie said. "I could keep score for you, I think. . . ."

Laura shook her head, still smiling. "No, but if *you'd* like to bowl. . . ."

Angie was aware of someone watching her from across the lanes. It was Sam all right; he had just come in. He didn't come over right away, and for a sinking moment Angie wondered what she would do if he just ignored her. What if he didn't recognize her or had completely forgotten her?

Moments later he paused uncertainly behind their seats. "Sharon?" he said on a faint questioning note. "Angie?"

She turned her head slowly. "Hello, Sam. I was hoping you'd be here." Smoothly she introduced him to Laura. "This is my friend Laura."

He shook hands and then turned back to Angie. "I thought you were kidding about coming back here." He shifted awkwardly from one foot to the other. "I mean, after I saw your picture in the paper and found out who you were and everything."

"Why don't you sit down, Sam?" Laura said suddenly. "I think I'll go have a cup of coffee." She got to her feet and smiled at Angie brightly. "You don't mind, do you, Angie?"

"No, I don't mind," Angie said, thinking of the three cups of coffee Laura had drunk with her dinner.

Sam slipped into the seat beside her and stared at her.

"Well," she said, when the silence had become embarrassing. "What do you think?"

He grinned, but not easily. "I like your own hair better. That wig looked pretty phony."

"It's a beautiful wig," she protested automatically. "Anyway it wasn't mine; it belongs to Laura."

"Are you really, I mean, can you really tell all that stuff like the paper says?"

"Sometimes I can," she said, "but I didn't know I'd ever see you again."

His eyes were puzzled.

"Anyway I'm glad you're here," she went on quickly, "because I wanted to say good-bye. To say thank you and good-bye."

"Thank me for what. For renting your shoes?"

She wanted to laugh, but she wanted to cry too.

"You're the first boy my own age I've ever talked to," she told him. "I'm fifteen, and I've never had a real date, like going bowling or to a movie or a school dance. That's why it was so special that you noticed me."

He looked amazed. "But that's crazy. You're famous. When I told my mother I'd met you at the bowling alley, she thought I was nuts."

Angie glanced across towards the coffee bar and could see that Laura was watching her. "Sam, I can't stay very long. We're flying home tonight, but I told you I'd come if I could." She touched his hand gently. "Maybe, maybe we'll meet again sometime."

"I could write to you," he said. "I'm not very good at writing, but I could try. I'd like to keep track of you."

"That's nice," she said. "I'd like that."

She opened her bag and found an envelope with her name and address. It was a letter she had received from one of the girls at school. She gave it to him.

"You can write to me there. If I'm traveling, they'll forward the letter."

"You haven't said you'll answer," he reminded her.

She looked at him searchingly. "I can't be sure I'll answer any more than you can be sure you'll write. I just hope we will."

Laura came back and slid into the seat on the other side of Angie. "Maybe we should get going, honey. There's still some packing." She shook hands with Sam and said she was glad to meet him. Then she got up and sauntered toward the door.

"The rest of the gang will be here in a few minutes," Sam said wistfully. "They aren't going to believe that you came."

"I really can't stay. Say hello to all of them for me. When you write to me, be sure to remind me to send some autographed pictures. Jeff had some made up for publicity. . . ." She was rattling on, as anxious to break away as she had been anxious to come. When she stood up, Sam got up too and followed her to the desk where Laura waited.

137

"Good-bye, Sam," she said. "Don't forget to write."

"Good-bye, Sharon-Angie," he said. "I think that's what I'll call you, Sharon-Angie."

They went out and got a taxi at the stand and were whirled back to the hotel.

"Do you think he *will* write?" Laura asked, when they got to their room.

"I don't know," Angie said. "Isn't it wonderful? I really *don't know*."

TEN

The plane lifted in the air and made a great sweep over the glitter that was Los Angeles. Across the aisle Jeff and Laura were talking softly. Angie looked down at the city and felt sadness squeeze her heart and tighten her throat. My father is there, she told herself. I didn't even see him, but he is there.

It was early in the morning when they reached the Kennedy airport, and dawn was still pearly and uncertain when they arrived at the apartment. They had dropped Laura off at her own place, declining her offer of breakfast in favor of getting home.

"This gal has had a hard week. She's going to relax and have fun for the entire weekend," Jeff declared. He didn't say anything about calling Laura later. Just kissed her lightly on the cheek and told her to watch it.

In the elevator going up to the apartment Angie found that she was yawning again. Yawning and yawning.

She was somewhat surprised to find the apartment lights on, and her mother up and dressed and waiting for her. "You didn't have to get up at this fantastic hour," Angie said, her face pressed against her mother's hair. Her mother didn't answer, just patted her, and Angie drew back, looking at her suspiciously. "Where's Grandmother?" she asked.

Her mother looked at Jeff. "You didn't tell her then?"

"I didn't think there was much point in upsetting her."

"Where's Grandmother?" Angie repeated, more loudly this time. "What happened?"

"She's going to be fine," her mother said soothingly. "The doctor says she'll probably be in the hospital another week or two. . . ."

"What happened?"

"She had a stroke, Angie. Saturday afternoon. We took her to the hospital, and she's doing fine. In a few weeks we can see about a nice convalescent home. . . ."

Angie stood very still. "You mean she isn't coming back here? Not ever?"

"Honey, it's too soon to tell," her mother replied. "Your grandmother isn't young. We want her to be where she'll get the best care possible."

"I'm tired," Angie said bleakly. "I think I want to go to bed now."

They took her to see her grandmother that afternoon. She was in a good hospital with crisp, efficient nurses and cheerful rooms. Although Grandmother looked as if she were asleep, the nurse said she was just resting. Only her eyes moved when Angie leaned over to kiss her.

I didn't even know, Angie found herself thinking. She's been lying here like this for almost a week, and I didn't even know.

"The nurse says she's doing as well as can be expected," Angie's mother whispered. Grandmother's tired eyes swung toward the voice and then back to Angie's face.

She touched her grandmother's hand that was lying limply at her side, and then squeezed the fingers firmly and warmly, but there was no answering pressure. "I'm sorry you've been ill, Grandmother. I didn't know."

Jeff was hovering in the background. He didn't come over to the bed or speak to her grandmother. Perhaps he felt that Grandmother wouldn't really care about seeing him.

Angie's mother went out to talk to the doctor, and Jeff followed her. Drawing a chair up to the bed, Angie sat close beside her grandmother talking softly. "You have to get well in a hurry, so we can get you out of this place, Grandma. After all, you're the one who winds us up and keeps us going, remember? Can you imagine what that apartment is like without you?"

A muscle twitched in the wrinkled cheek as if Grandma wanted to smile, but couldn't. One side of her face was absolutely without expression. Partial paralysis. In the car coming across town her mother had used some such term.

"You aren't to worry about anything except getting well. I'll talk to the doctor myself and make him see that you *have* to come home. We'll get you a wheel chair, if that's what you'll need, and we can have a nurse come in and look after you."

Her grandmother made a sound that wasn't really a word, and then her eyes dimmed with tears.

"Don't try to talk," Angie said fiercely. "Don't try to do anything. Just lie there and concentrate on getting well." She picked up the limp hand and held it for a moment against her cheek; her throat was thick with tears.

"It seems so funny to see you lying in bed in the middle of the day," she went on, as soon as she could trust her voice. "Do you know when I was a little girl, when we lived in the old house on Chelsea Street and you had your own little room, I used to think you never went to bed. You were busy when I went to sleep at night and busy when I got up in the morning, and I thought you never undressed and went to bed like other people. I remember that it was a big shock to me when we moved and you slept in the same room with me and Celia. I used to tiptoe over and watch you breathing in the middle of the night. You looked like a stranger when you were asleep."

The dark pain-filled eyes were watching her attentively.

Her mother came back into the room and touched Angie's shoulder. "We'd better go, Angie. The chances are she doesn't even know we're here."

Angie looked up quickly. "Of course, she knows. She can't talk, but she knows we're here." She leaned over and kissed her grandmother's cheek, smoothed the sparse hair back from her forehead. "We'll be back to see you later on, Grandma. I wish there was something we could bring you. How about some bright flowers? You could look at them, and they'd make you feel more cheerful. Okay?"

Her mother came over and patted the mound of covers gently. "Poor Mama," she said. "It hurts seeing her like this. . . ."

They followed Jeff out of the room and down the corridor, but before he left Angie paused in the doorway to glance back. She was certain that her grandmother's eyes followed her, that they were trying to tell her something.

In the elevators a little girl stared at Angie, and then nudged the woman standing beside her. "It *is* her," the whisper floated after Angie as Jeff ushered them out on the first floor. "It is too."

In the car Jeff turned his head and looked at Angie uncertainly. "I've made an appointment for you, Angie, with Doctor Bellamy. I talked to him this morning, and even though he doesn't have regular office hours he's agreed to see you at two o'clock."

"But why? I'm not sick."

"We want to find out what's causing those headaches. Your blackout last Saturday may have something to do with them, or they may be completely unrelated. Doctor Bellamy is an avid student of psychic phenomena. He has a theory that your nervous system may be hooked up a little differently from the rest of us peasants." Jeff went on talking lightly and firmly, as if to ward off any objections Angie might offer. "Anyway it won't hurt to see what he has to say."

They went back to the apartment where Celia was getting dressed to go out. She greeted Angie with her usual lack of enthusiasm, but when Angie asked about her role in the school play she was pleased. "Oh, it's a great part, Angie. Something I really can get my teeth into. I may decide to turn professional. Mr. Kruger says I have a lot of talent. . . ."

Angie listened and nodded and smiled. Still, when Celia finally stopped for breath, she couldn't resist asking, "Celia? Did you ask about Grandmother? We've been talking about other things so fast that I didn't notice."

Celia's pretty face clouded. "Well, how is she?"

"She can't talk; she can't even move. She just lies there with her eyes looking at nothing. Have you been up to the hosptial to see her?"

"I've been busy," Celia snapped. "Anyway what could I do at the hospital? Sit and hold her hand?"

"That might do for a start," Angie said calmly.

"Oh, for heaven's sake, she's an old lady, Angie. She'll probably die pretty soon. Of course, I'm *sorry*. . . ." The blue eyes filled with easy tears. "But what possible good could it do if I went up there and got myself all upset?"

"No good at all," Angie said quietly. "I'm sorry I mentioned the subject."

Angie liked Doctor Bellamy at once. He didn't look anything like a doctor. He was skinny and awkward with enormous hands and feet, and he looked as if his clothes might have been picked haphazardly off a rack with no particular attention paid to size and fit. But he had a smile that lighted all his features, and his brown eyes were warm and interested.

"So you are Angie," he said, when the nurse showed her into his consultation room. He turned from the window where he had been looking out and crossed quickly to her side. "I know the papers insist you are only fourteen, but I expected you to be older."

"I *am* older," Angie said. "I'm fifteen. I just had a birthday last week."

"Did you come alone?" Doctor Bellamy asked, going back to his chair behind the big desk. "Or is Jeff waiting for you?"

"Mother came with me," Angie said. "She insisted." Then she slanted a quick smile at the man across the desk. "She wants to find out what kind of doctor you are."

He grinned. "One of those, hmm?"

"What kind *are* you?" Angie asked.

He shrugged. "Let's just say I have a degree in psychology that I find most helpful in my business. A psychiatrist I'm not." He held out his hand to her suddenly. "Come here, Angie. Jeff said something about a series of headaches. Let's look at your eyes."

The examination was as informal as saying "Ahhhh" to see if she had a sore throat. He drew the blinds and made Angie open and close her eyes and look into a bright little light while he checked her reflexes.

"I'll want to do some extensive tests next week," he said at last, "but for now we'll go on the assumption that your headaches are not caused by any pressure on the optic nerves." He went to rearrange the blinds, and Angie returned to her chair.

"Let's talk," Doctor Bellamy said mildly. "Let's

145

just talk about this remarkable gift of yours, and what you can do with it. And what it can do with you." He leaned toward her coaxingly. "I suppose Jeff has warned you that I'm interested in psychic phenomena."

"He said you were a student," Angie said demurely.

The doctor made a face. He half turned in his chair and indicated a row of books on a nearby shelf. "See those? I read everything I can get my hands on about the subject and everything related to it. Cryptesthesia has always fascinated me, but it wasn't until I became a doctor that I learned to study it as a scientific possibility."

"Cryptesthesia," Angie repeated the word slowly. "I'm not sure I know what it means."

"It's what you have, Angie. A power by which we become aware of facts unknown to us in either the present or the future."

She nodded and settled back in her chair. "Oh," she said.

"Are you familiar with poltergeist activity, Angie? With physical disturbances? Have you ventured into any form of spiritualism at all?"

"You mean getting messages from people who have died?" She leaned forward, looking at him intently. "Is that why you really wanted to see me, Doctor Bellamy? To see if I could tell you anything about" — she paused and then spoke slowly — "about your wife?"

His eyes flickered for a moment, and then he smiled. "My dear Angie, I was asking a question, hopefully. My wife has been dead for a good many years, and I have never been able to contact her.

I'll admit I've made several attempts. . . ." He got up quickly and went to the door to call the nurse. "I think we'll do a couple of tests on Angie this afternoon. The scans will have to wait until a day next week when the technicians are here. Set up an appointment for Tuesday or Wednesday, will you, Miss Casey?"

He was abruptly a professional man again. Angie knew that he was a little embarrassed, and she couldn't help wishing there were some tactful way to let him know that she didn't really mind that his interest in her was not so much what he could do to help *her* as what she might be able to do for him.

The tests were long and tiring. Doctor Bellamy succeeded in locating the exact spot behind her ear where the headaches seemed to strike. He made brisk unintelligible remarks, which the nurse dutifully recorded. He asked if she took any medication, and Angie said just a few aspirin and some tranquilizers when she was especially tense.

"What do you mean tense?" he snapped.

Angie smiled at him, wanting them to be friends again. "Oh, you know, when I'm nervous and afraid I might not do very well before an audience."

The doctor and nurse glanced at one another. "Who prescribed the tranquilizers?"

She shrugged. "I really don't know. Jeff got them for me. Sometimes Mother uses them, too."

The doctor looked grim. "I'll have to talk with Jeff. Miss Casey, would you contact Jeff Granger and ask him to come in to see me some time Monday?"

147

Angie was sorry she had even mentioned the tranquilizers.

"When you have these headaches, is it always before a performance?"

She thought, trying to remember. "Not always. Sometimes I wake up at night with a headache. Then take an aspirin."

"An aspirin, not a sleeping tablet?"

"No" — she shook her head — "just the aspirin."

"And does the headache always go away?"

"Not always, sometimes I still have it in the morning."

"It could be simple eyestrain, or it could be something much more serious. We'll know better when we have the scans. Have you ever worn glasses, Angie?"

"No, never."

He nodded. "Well, maybe you should."

When they were going back to the apartment Angie remembered the flowers for her grandmother. They stopped at a florist, and she ordered a large bouquet. "Don't make it look too much like an arrangement," she told the woman in charge. "Just like I'd gone out and picked them and jammed them down in a vase, okay?"

The woman looked amazed, but she nodded her head.

Angie's mother gave the address and Grandmother's name and wrote the check while Angie scrawled a message on the card. "I love you, Angie," she wrote in large round letters so that the nurse would be able to hold up the card and Grandmother could read it.

"All that money for a bunch of flowers that will

be gone in two or three days," Angie's mother grumbled, when they went out to look for a cab.

Angie stared at her. "You and Jeff are always telling me that I should get more fun out of having money. You're always wanting me to buy new records and sweaters and junk."

Her mother looked harassed. "But Angie, it's normal for a fifteen-year-old to want those things. We want you to be happy."

"I'm happy," Angie said serenely. "I guess I'm just not very normal."

The next week was filled with school, visits to the hospital, and the appointments with Doctor Bellamy. The doctor had talked to Jeff about the tranquilizers, but Jeff just laughed off his concern by saying that they were tablets he picked up without a prescription in the drugstore. One day while she was in the doctor's office a couple of other men came in to talk to her.

"Angie, you could be a big help to us. We're doing a great deal of work at the university where Doctor Kincaid and I are teaching. Do you suppose you could let us run some tests on you?"

"I don't know," Angie said. "I went to a university for tests two or three different times. Once they tried to make me go into a trance, but I couldn't. . . ." She looked from one man to the other, and her mouth quirked into a little smile. "They *thought* I was going into a trance, but instead I fell asleep. It was pretty embarrassing for everyone."

Doctor Bellamy interrupted. "These men might be able to help you, Angie. They could explain a lot of the things that trouble you. Like being sure

149

that your father was in the audience in Los Angeles. . ."

"But he *was* there. I'm sure he was."

Finally she told them she would be happy to submit to the tests if Jeff and her mother were agreeable. "But not during the day. I go to school from nine till two."

Jeff turned down the offer flatly. He didn't explain to Angie or her mother; he just said no. The doctors were upset, and even Doctor Bellamy said the decision seemed like a criminal waste, but Jeff was unshakable.

That night he came to the apartment and told Angie that he almost had completed the second book. It undoubtedly would be even more popular than the first, since she was so much more well known now. And there was a movie offer. One of the major studios was considering doing a movie based on the book. "You'll be too busy, honey. From now on we pick and choose. No more of these one-night stands."

The same night, while Jeff was still there, a collect call for Angie came from Los Angeles. Angie was the one who answered the phone, and she accepted the call immediately.

Dragging the telephone cord behind her, she walked into the kitchen. "Hello," she said softly. "Hello, Father."

He sounded just the same, exactly the same. "Hello, Angie. It's been a long time, hasn't it?"

"Yes." Her throat felt tight, because just hearing his voice made her able to see him clearly. "Are you all right?" she said. "Are you happy?"

There was a little pause before he answered

150

her. "Is anyone ever really happy? I have my work and some friends and a place to hang my hat. I read about you and have a whole collection of articles that have been written about you. Whenever I get drunk, I brag about your being my daughter, but no one believes me so that's all right."

"Last week," she said, "when I was in Los Angeles, why didn't you come to see me?"

There was a faint smile in his voice. "I tried, Angela. I tried to get into the theatre, but I almost landed in jail, so I got myself some papers and stood on the corner by your hotel, and a couple of times I had glimpses of you. Once you were with a pretty young woman, and you stood talking for quite a while before the doorman called you a cab. I almost spoke to you then. . . ."

"Why didn't you?" Angie wasn't even aware that tears were sliding down her cheek until she tasted the salt on her lips. "Why didn't you?"

"It was enough to see you, baby. To be sure that you were the fine young woman the papers said you were. I couldn't possibly add anything to your life, and I don't want to disrupt it again." She knew by the husky note in his voice that he was crying too.

"Do you want to speak to Mother?" she asked.

His answering "no" was almost automatic. "No, I just wanted to talk to you. To hear your voice and let you know I think of you and miss you very much." He hesitated for such a long time that she thought he might have hung up, and then he spoke again hurriedly. "There is one small favor you can do for me, honey. I hate to ask, but — " Again he hesitated.

"What?" Angie asked anxiously. "What can I do for you, Father?"

She thought she heard a little sigh, and then he spoke very gently. "You still say your prayers, don't you? Well, say one for me now and then, will you, Angel?"

She stared at the phone unbelievingly when the faint click indicated that he had hung up.

As she walked into the living room both her mother and Jeff looked up from the TV show they were watching. Jeff's eyes narrowed when he saw that she had been crying, but her mother was the one who spoke. "Angie, what's wrong, dear?" Angie just shook her head, and she rushed on. "That telephone call, it was bad news, wasn't it? Your grandmother . . ."

"It wasn't Grandmother. It was Father."

Something flickered for a moment in her mother's eyes. Hope? Fear? Panic?

"Where is he?"

"He's in Los Angeles. He just wanted to know . . . he just wanted to be sure we were all right."

"Why didn't you call me?" Her mother's voice went up sharply. "Why didn't you call me, Angie?"

"He didn't want me to . . . to disturb you."

"He must have called for some reason. He wouldn't call just for nothing after all these years." She stood up, looking pale and worried, but angry too. "Angie, I *insist* on knowing what he said."

Jeff got to his feet and spoke quickly. "I'm going home, Jessie. This is between you and Angie.

It has nothing to do with me." He started for the door, and then looked back at them. "You must have known this could happen. Angie's a celebrity. It's perfectly natural that her father should want to ride on the gravy train, too. He'll call again."

"No," Angie spoke without thinking. "No, it isn't like that at all. He just wanted to be sure we were all right." They both stared at her, not believing her for a second. "He saw me in Los Angeles. He waited by the hotel and watched me. He said that he didn't want to disrupt our lives again."

"You should have called me," her mother repeated flatly. "You should have called me."

"Maybe not," Jeff said briskly. "Maybe this is for the best. I'll talk to the lawyer tomorrow and find out if he has any legal grounds after all this time."

Angie stood miserably and shook her head. The tears were still sliding down her cheeks, and she wished she could forget that her father had said, "There is one small favor you can do for me, honey," before he had changed his mind and asked her to remember him in her prayers.

That next weekend she and Jeff went to Philadelphia for an interview and to make some tapes. Just before she left she called and ordered more flowers for her grandmother. She took them to the hospital herself and sat and talked with her grandmother until the time came to go to the train.

The nurse appeared in the doorway several times while Angie sat by the bed, stroking Grandmother's limp hand and telling her about the trip to

Los Angeles, about Doctor Bellamy and the doctors from the university who wanted her to be a guinea pig. "But Jeff told them no, because he has a lot of other things lined up for me. Another book and a movie and a lot of exciting guest spots. And besides, there's school. Jeff says that now that I'm established I can go to school and not have a tutor. He'll arrange the appearances for weekends, and we'll commute. . . ."

She didn't know whether everything she was saying got through to her grandmother. Even though she held her grandmother's hand and looked deeply into her eyes, she couldn't seem to find the key that would unlock the things her grandmother was trying to tell her.

She got up and rearranged the flowers, placing them so that her grandmother could see them without turning her eyes. "Aren't they lovely? I was so glad they had daisies. Mother says you used to love them and that you used to make little daisy crowns for Celia and me to wear in our hair."

Jeff came in after a while, and she had to leave. Angie dropped a swift kiss on her grandmother's faded cheek. "Good-bye, Grandmother. We'll see you in a few days."

ELEVEN

The trip to Philadelphia was almost without incident. Jeff seemed preoccupied 'and no one on the train recognized Angie, but in the taxi going to the hotel the cab driver kept peering at her in his rearview mirror.

"Hey, aren't you the kid we've been seeing on TV? The one who can read minds and stuff like that?" When Angie smiled and nodded, he beamed with excitement. "Wait'll I tell the wife about this. She'll flip. My wife is a real TV nut. Watches day and night." He swerved around a truck skillfully, and then looked at Angie again. "How about telling me something about myself? So I can have something to brag about."

"She'll predict an accident unless you keep your eyes on the road," Jeff said shortly, but Angie laughed and leaned forward, studying the lines of the man's homely face.

"You don't look anything like your picture," she said. "I guess it was taken a long time ago."

He shook his head. "We gotta have 'em renewed every couple of years."

Angie nodded. "I guess it's just that you weren't so happy when the picture was taken. Happy the way you are now, I mean."

The man looked startled. "Is that right?"

"I think you're happy now, because . . . because your wife is young and beautiful and she loves you."

The cab swerved, and the driver righted it instantly. He muttered something explosive under his breath, and his eyes, when they finally met Angie's in the rearview mirror, were filled with awe.

As he pulled up before the hotel he flipped off the meter and turned to stare at Angie in the back seat. The doorman came over to open the door, and Jeff bounced out of the cab impatiently.

"How much?" he asked, his hand already reaching for his wallet.

The driver shook his head. "Skip it. No charge."

Angie let Jeff help her out of the cab and smiled at the man. "Thank you," she said. "I hope you stay very happy."

In the lobby they met a girl who had been sent over by the studio to chaperone Angie. Jeff left them in the coffee shop having lunch while he went on about his business. The girl's name was Jan something or other. She turned out to be the daughter of one of the producers, and she was highly skeptical of Angie's talents.

Angie listened to her talk and agreed with whatever Jan said pleasantly enough. She agreed that ESP was much overrated and not scientific at all, but a combination of superstition and trickery. She agreed that mind reading was impossible and that people who correctly foretold earthquakes, assassinations, and presidential elections were either enormously lucky or well informed.

She talked so much that Angie found herself getting another headache. "Perhaps we could go up to my room," she said after a while. "I'd like to unpack, and I really should call home. My grandmother is in the hospital, and I like to keep in touch."

"You mean you can't look into your crystal ball and see how she's getting along?" Jan asked slyly.

"No, I can't," Angie said shortly. "I don't even own a crystal ball."

Jan paid the check and followed Angie into the elevator, still wearing her smug superior little smile.

Upstairs, in the room, Angie yawned and spoke very gently. "But if I did have a crystal ball I could see that you got a traffic ticket on the way over here, and you're worried about how you're going to tell your father." She went into the bathroom and closed the door on Jan's shocked face.

She hadn't been able to resist, but afterward she was sorry because Jan Logan became an instant believer and pestered Angie for the rest of the time they were together. "Tell me what will happen.

Tell me whom I'll marry. Tell me, tell me."

Angie finally escaped by lying down and pretending to take a nap, but she was aware of the other girl buzzing about the room like an impatient mosquito waiting for Angie to open her eyes.

She told Jeff about Jan when he came to pick her up for an interview a little later. "I don't know whether I'll be able to stand that girl," she informed Jeff grumpily. "I made the mistake of telling her she just got a speeding ticket, and now she's prodding me for information every minute."

He looked at her with mild amusement. "How did you happen to tell her that? Did she ask you?"

"No, but she was being so smug and smart . . ." Angie paused and grinned. "I expect I was just showing off. But it was like the taxi driver this morning. She was *thinking* about that ticket so hard that it was all around her like a fog."

"And the taxi driver was thinking about his beautiful young wife?"

"Oh, yes. Except I don't think she's as young and beautiful as *he* thinks she is. I don't think she's a very nice person at all, and it's too bad because he's so happy. She turned her head and looked at Jeff almost reproachfully. "Couldn't you feel how happy he was?"

Jeff shook his head. "Afraid not, honey. Not until he told me to skip the taxi fare. And then I thought he was sick."

The interview was like a dozen other interviews. Angie wasn't exactly bored; she just felt detached. But then a name was mentioned that jarred her to awareness. "Did you say— I'm sorry, I was thinking of something else — did you mention Amir Kandesh Akbar?"

"Why, yes." The man who was conducting the interview turned toward her quickly. "He died recently, you know. Did you ever meet him, Angie?"

"Yes, a long time ago. I'd almost forgotten. How did he die?"

"Under very strange circumstances, they say. He was found in a coma, and evidently there was no medical explanation for what had happened, although some people suggested self-hypnosis. At any rate, the coma lasted for about ten days, and then he died. I've heard he was a very brilliant man, but I never was fortunate enough to know him."

Angie swallowed hard. She felt immeasurably sad without knowing why. She had come in contact with the man so briefly and so long ago that she couldn't account for the strength of her reaction.

Going back to the hotel in the cab, she tried to tell Jeff about Doctor Akbar. "Jeff, do you believe in transference? I mean, the way the Hindus believe? That a person can leave his body and go away, and then come back to it?"

He looked at her thoughtfully. "Do you believe in it?"

"I don't know. But suppose a person *could* do such a thing. Suppose I left my body and went away — to look for my father, maybe — and then someone thought I was dead and buried me."

"Hey, whoa," Jeff said in alarm. "If you must know, I don't think it's even remotely possible. Is that what's bothering you? Thinking that this Akbar character might have taken off and come back to find his body gone?"

Angie studied him for a long moment, and then smiled. "Don't look so upset. As you say, I don't think it's remotely possible either."

They went back to the room, and while Angie changed her clothes Jeff had a talk with Jan Logan. Angie didn't hear what he said, but it must have been effective because there were no more questions.

Getting to sleep was difficult. She took her tranquilizers and even one of the mild sleeping tablets Doctor Bellamy had prescribed, but she was as wide awake as ever. At two o'clock she awakened from a restless doze and took another tranquilizer. Then, to be on the safe side, she took two more sleeping tablets. Across the room she could see the sleeping form of Jan Logan, but the girl didn't stir.

Angie slipped back into bed and stared at the ceiling, willing herself to relax, but there was a strange pounding in her head and she was troubled by the overpowering fragrance of many flowers. Carefully she lifted herself on one elbow and peered through the semidarkness at the dressing table. Strange she hadn't noticed the flowers before. Perhaps the studio sent them, and Jan had forgotten to point them out. They didn't look like the kind of flowers a studio would send, though; they were an old-fashioned arrangement of tulips, small chrysanthemums, and daisies . . . small yellow daisies. . . . The flowers looked so familiar, so terribly familiar.

She started to get up, and then heard a voice speaking her name, softly and insistently. "Angie, Angie, Angie."

I am afraid, she told herself clearly and lucidly. I don't know why, but I'm terribly afraid. And then there was darkness. She was in a room that was strange and yet familiar. There was a bed with a silent mound. There was the bouquet of old-fashioned flowers, and there was a quiet figure standing by the window.

Grandmother turned her head and looked at Angie. "I've been calling and calling," she said in an impatient, demanding voice. "What took you so long?"

Angie moved closer, wishing that she dared turn on the lights. "I'm sorry, Grandmother. I was asleep. But I'm here now."

"All this gallivanting around," Grandmother said crossly. "It isn't a normal life for a youngster."

In the faint light from the open doorway Angie could hardly distinguish her grandmother's features. She dimly heard the faraway sound of heels tapping, the faint buzz of a telephone that was quickly answered, the sliding hiss of elevator doors.

Her grandmother seemed to hear the noises, too. She moved a step closer, and her hand was firm and sure on Angie's arm. "There isn't much time, Angie, and there is so much I want to say to you."

"Tell me now," Angie said, and sat down on the very edge of the chair by the window.

"I'm afraid for you," her grandmother said simply. "I've been afraid for a long time, but now I know that I must tell you what I feel. It's true that you have a great gift. I've denied it to you, but never to myself. A God-given gift, Angie, and you must use it to help people. Not to grow rich and famous, but to help. The men who wanted to study you were good scientific men, who really need the information you can give them. There is so much to be explored. . . ."

"I know," Angie said.

Her grandmother glanced nervously toward the doorway. There was the sound of wheels coming down the corridor. "You won't ever be an ordinary human being, Angie, because you have this special awareness, but you can be a vessel for good. Do you understand what I am trying to tell you?"

"Yes," Angie said. Then she turned and watched as a couple of young boys trundled a cart into the room, flicking on the overhead light at the same time. They stopped short in surprise seeing Angie.

"Hey, I'm sorry," one of the boys said awkwardly. "I didn't think anyone was here. We came to get the . . . the. . ." He gestured toward the bed. "Is it okay?"

"She was my grandmother," Angie said. "Yes, it's okay."

She turned her back and looked out the window as they removed the mound from the bed. She didn't glance around even when she heard the wheels creaking once more and knew that they had gone away. Her eyes were dim with tears as she picked up a small circle of flowers from the bedside table. A daisy wreath, her grandmother had fashioned a daisy wreath. . . .

Angie was aware of excited voices and opened her eyes painfully. Jeff's face was there and Jan's and someone else's, a face she didn't know.

Jeff's hands were on her shoulders. shaking her gently. "Angie, are you okay? You've been having a nightmare. Jan tried to wake you when you started moaning, but she said you were absolutely limp, so she called me and I got the house doctor." He turned and glanced at the man. "You had us all pretty scared."

The doctor was holding the bottle of pills that Doctor Bellamy had given her. He looked sober. "The sleeping tablets may contain something she isn't able to tolerate. It's most unusual. Do I have your permission to have these analyzed?"

"Yes, certainly, but you'll find that everything is in order."

"I hope so," the doctor said. "But two medicines sometimes work against each other with strange results, sometimes tragic results. Why should this child have to take tranquilizers and sleeping tablets?"

"She's subject to headaches and at times is very nervous," Jeff said hastily. "Well, Doctor Madison, I appreciate your coming so quickly, but I really think Angie will be okay now."

Angie watched as he gently edged the man toward the door and got rid of him. Jan was sitting on the side of her bed. She was wearing her bathrobe and slippers and a very dazed expression. Poor Jan, she wouldn't forget this weekend soon. In later years she'd probably tell her children about the time she was chaperone to Angie Scofield. "Maybe you don't remember hearing about her, but she used to be a mystic. I wonder whatever happened to her. She sort of dropped out of sight. . . ."

Jeff came back to her bedside and smiled down at Angie. "That's better," he said. "Do me a favor, sweetie, and don't ever take these pills again." He put his hand on her forehead awkwardly. "You feel okay?"

"I feel fine," she said, and closed her eyes so he wouldn't see the tears.

They went home the next morning. Jeff canceled a telecast that might have been very important. She never knew whether he knew about her grandmother; she never asked.

But when they went home, when her mother met them at the door in tears and told them that Grandmother had died sometime during the night, she shed the tears that were expected of her. Celia cried, too. At Grandmother's funeral she cried harder than anyone.

Angie didn't shed a tear.

There were a lot of people at the funeral; some of them were complete strangers. Angie knew without being told that they came to get a glimpse of her.

Afterward they went back to the apartment, and Jeff returned with them. To a casual observer they probably looked like a family, Angie told herself a little wistfully.

Celia went almost at once to the telephone and called one of her friends. She talked for a long time while Angie's mother went to the kitchen to start some coffee and Jeff moved restlessly up and down the big living room.

Angie sat very still in one corner of the sofa, her hands folded quietly in her lap. Once Jeff paused in his pacing and gazed at her with concern in his eyes. "Do you want to lie down for a while, honey? You're probably beat."

"No, I don't want to lie down. I'm fine. But I

hope you don't have any place special to go this afternoon, Jeff. I'd like to have you stay. I think we ought to have a talk."

He smiled at her. "Of course, I'll stay if you want me. My time is your time. You know that."

Celia turned from the phone. "I'm going over to Paula's for a while. Her cousin's there, and she's been dying to have me meet him." Then her eyes met Angie's, and her chin came up. "After all, what good would it do Grandmother to have me sit around and *brood*? We have to go on living no matter how terrible we feel inside."

"You're probably right," Angie said. "Grandmother would hate to have you mourn for her."

Celia looked suspicious. "What kind of crack is that? She wasn't just *your* grandmother, you know. She was mine, too."

"I know, it must have been a great comfort to her," Angie couldn't help saying, but she was sorry almost before Celia had flounced out of the room. Celia couldn't help being the way she was.

Her mother came in with a tray of sandwiches and some mugs of coffee. She had been crying again, and Angie was sorry. For the first time she remembered that her mother would miss her grandmother more than any of them. For years and years her grandmother had been there saying, "Don't bother with that, Jessie. I'll take care of it." Or, "Why don't you run along, Jessie? This will just take me a minute."

"It probably isn't very good coffee," her mother said unsteadily. "I seem to be all thumbs these days."

Jeff helped her with the tray and offered no

165

objection when she poured a mug of coffee for Angie. Perhaps they were all remembering that Grandmother had said if Angie was old enough to support the family she was old enough to drink coffee.

She sat holding the mug between her two hands, feeling the warmth and comfort even before she sipped the coffee.

Jeff helped himself to a sandwich and dropped in the chair opposite Angie. His eyes were troubled. "About that talk . . ." he suggested very gently.

Her mother glanced at her and then at Jeff. She picked up her coffee and sat down beside Angie, letting her hand rest briefly on Angie's knee as if to remind her that Mother was there.

"I don't know exactly how to say this," Angie began very slowly. "I want to say it properly so that you'll understand, both of you, because I love you and I know that you love me."

"Of course, we love you," Angie's mother said, but Jeff said nothing. She could feel him waiting.

"I've been thinking a lot about what I want to do with my life," Angie went on. "Not just today and tomorrow and next month, but all my life." She paused and then looked directly at Jeff. "Maybe it's too late for me to stop being Angie, but I want to try. I really want to try, Jeff. I'd like to go to the university with Professor Carlton and be part of his study. Afterward, when people have started to forget that I'm Angie, the girl mystic, I'd like to go away somewhere and attend a regular school." She stopped and waited.

Her mother spoke into the ticking silence. "Honey, you don't really mean this. You're upset

166

about Grandmother, and what you need is a good long vacation. You could arrange one, couldn't you, Jeff? We might even go to the Caribbean, or we could . . ."

She stopped talking, because neither of the others was paying any attention to her. Jeff had leaned forward, and his eyes were searching Angie's face. "Are you telling us that you aren't happy?"

"I'm not unhappy," she told him. "At least, I don't think I'm unhappy, but sometimes I envy the other kids. Like the ones at the bowling alley in Los Angeles. Sam wrote to me, and I answered the letter, and I thought we were going to have a nice easy friendship that had nothing to do with my being Angie. But then he didn't write back, so I wrote again, and this time his letter was different, more like a fan letter."

Angie could see that Jeff was listening and really trying to understand, so she went on. "It was the same when Father called. He didn't call just to be sure we were all right. I think he called because he wanted some of the money. He must know that I'm making a great deal of money, don't you think so?"

Jeff nodded. "I'm sure he does. What then, Angie?"

"I don't know. I just know that I'm terribly tired. Sometimes I don't even feel that I know who I am. I'm just someone standing there watching Angie Scofield go through her tricks. I don't know what's real and what's pretend. I think that's why I get the headaches."

Her mother's hand touched hers. "There's something else, isn't there?"

"Yes, I didn't want to tell you right away. It

167

was something I wanted to keep to myself. But that night" — her eyes sought Jeff's again — "the night I took the sleeping pills and you thought I'd taken an overdose, I wasn't there, Jeff. I was with Grandmother. I was with her in that hospital room. I was there when they came up from the morgue and took her body away. You can ask the boys at the hospital. One of them talked to me."

"Honey, it was just a dream," Angie's mother broke in quickly. "I have the same sort of dreams myself, so real that I could swear everything really happened."

"I was there," Angie said. "I didn't even try to be there, but I heard her calling me, and I could smell the flowers I'd sent her. I was *there*, in the room with her." She looked from Jeff's listening face to her mother's shocked one. "I talked to her and she talked to me, and then they came and took her away and I went back." She paused and swallowed. "It scared me. Not seeing Grandmother and talking to her, because of course I couldn't be afraid of her, but I couldn't help thinking. . . . What if someday I go away like that and can't find my way back? What could happen to me then?"

"My God," Jeff said softly. He used the words as a prayer not as a curse.

She waited for him to say something more, but her mother spoke instead. "It's just what I said, Angie. You're really tired. What you need is a vacation. Don't you remember how upset we all were when Stacy died? But then you went away to that lovely camp, and when you came back you'd forgotten all about it."

Angie gazed at her steadily. "No, I didn't forget all about it. Did you?"

"No, of course not." Her mother looked ready to cry. "But Angie, you can't all of a sudden decide you don't want to be Angie. You *are* Angie." She patted Angie's hand, and then continued less excitedly. "You don't realize it, but you'd miss all the excitement. You'd miss having people stop you on the street for your autograph. You'd miss having lovely clothes and all that money in the trust fund for your education. You'd even miss this apartment. . . ." Her mother stared at Jeff then, almost pleadingly.

"Your mother is right, you know," Jeff said. "There are a lot of things to consider. In a few more years your future will be secure. There is this talk about using the new book for a movie. I've even had some feelers about whether you might want to play yourself." He tilted his head to one side and shrugged. "Most people would jump at the chance of being in the movies, but not my girl." She said nothing, and he went on in the same carefully expressionless voice. "I turned down the syndicated column. I thought it was too soon."

Angie could sense Jeff's anguish. Her decision would be harder for him than any of them. "Jeff, I'm sorry. Truly sorry."

"What is that supposed to mean?" her mother broke in. "You're *sorry!* Jeff has practically devoted his life to you. He gave up a perfectly good job. . . ."

"Be quiet," Jeff said so mildly that her mother stopped talking immediately. "Look at me, Angie." She raised her eyes, and he gave her a smile that must have cost him a great effort. "Let's forget the material things for a moment. Those things are

169

important, but we'll forget them for the time being. Okay?" She barely nodded, and he went on. "I have to know *why*. This isn't just your future; it's mine, too. Even if you succeed in cutting yourself off from Angie, the girl mystic, my life is irrevocably tangled up with hers." He leaned over and touched her hand. "I wouldn't have it any other way, but that's the truth of the matter."

Angie nodded, not understanding, but feeling close to tears.

"So I have to have a good reason. You say you saw your grandmother and talked to her. Did she suggest this decision?"

Angie shook her head; her throat felt dry. "No, it's hard to remember, because . . . because they were coming to take her away. There wasn't much time. She said I had a great gift and that it should be used to help people. She said I could help those men at the university. . . ."

Jeff sighed. "All right. Now let's suppose something else. If you hadn't seen your grandmother, talked to her, would you still want to do this? Is it what you would like your life to be?"

"Yes," she said promptly. "Grandmother said something else that I'd almost forgotten. She said I'll always have this special awareness and that I could be a vessel for good."

Jeff stood up abruptly. "I'm sure you can, Angie. You've never been anything else." He turned to Angie's mother, who was ready to protest. "It isn't the end of the world, Jessie. It just calls for a little soul-searching. So how about another cup of coffee?

170

In the end the arrangements were relatively simple. Jeff canceled all the engagements and issued a statement to the effect that Angie Scofield had retired. Some of the newspapers hinted that the announcement was yet another publicity stunt.

"The money will be rolling in for a good many years," Jeff told Angie and her mother the day he returned to them the contract Angie's mother had signed so many years before. "There are the book royalties and the movie sale and subsidiary rights on a lot of things we haven't even considered. I think it would be a good idea to sublet the apartment and find a house in the suburbs. It will take time for Angie to stop being the girl mystic, but with patience . . . Well, people do forget."

Celia thought they were all crazy and said so in no uncertain terms. "I think it's the stupidest thing I ever heard of. All that money down the drain just because she wants to be temperamental. If she's tired and upset, why can't she take a couple of months off and go to Europe or something? Why does she have to ruin everything for the rest of us?"

Angie didn't try to explain. There was no reasoning with Celia. She tried to comfort herself with the certain knowledge that before very long Celia would be leaving them. She really wouldn't miss Celia, and she had an idea that her mother wouldn't either. Celia didn't care what happened to anyone but Celia.

They found a house in a small town upstate. A beautiful little town and a small perfect house. "Grandmother would have loved it," Angie said the first time they went to see the place.

While her mother and the real-estate man were signing all the necessary papers Angie waited in the office. There was a newspaper lying face up on a coffee table, and Angie picked it up and glanced at the headlines. "Girl still missing. Owner of bloodstained car held for investigation." The picture of a frightened young man looked out of the page at Angie, and she felt her heart stir with sympathy.

The story was brief. The young man claimed that he and the girl had quarreled, that she had opened the car door and run into a service-station rest room and that when she had failed to reappear after an hour he had called the service-station attendant to break the door and found that the girl had left through a rear window. The service-station attendant corroborated his testimony, but there was no explanation for the bloodstains and why the girl hadn't returned home. Meanwhile, the police . . .

Angie turned the page to read further and saw the picture of the girl. Of côurse, he hadn't killed her. He loved her. She was enjoying the commotion she was causing, but today she would be in touch with her parents and admit that she had run away, that she was half-ashamed to come back after all the trouble she had caused.

"Reading about the Martin girl?" A man passing through the office glanced at the paper and shook his head. "Bad business, that. Looks like the boy will hang for sure."

Angie started to protest, and then realized the boy didn't need her. Maybe, though, she could help people in similar trouble in the future.

"You'll like the school we have here," the real-estate man told Angie, when they emerged from the office into the sunshine. "Got a new gym and everything."

"It will probably be fun living in a small town," Angie's mother said so happily that one would almost think the move had been her idea in the first place.

The real-estate man went to the car, and Angie thought of something. "I'm going to have my hair cut," she said suddenly. "Can I have it cut terribly short, so that I almost look like a boy?"

"I'm afraid it will take more than a haircut to make you look like a boy," her mother said indulgently. "And honey, you can't make people forget Angie, even if you change your hair. But then someday you may want them to remember. You may want to travel again and have people ask for your autograph. You may *want* to be Angie again."

"Maybe." Angie shook her hair back and brushed a stray lock away from her cheek. "Maybe after a long time. When I'm able to decide what to do with my life, who I really am."

They got into the agent's car and drove back to the railroad station. When the man let them out, a woman smiled at her and said, "Hello, Angie." Of course, Angie never had seen the woman before.

They told Celia all about the house, but she wasn't terribly interested. She would have to transfer from her school where all her friends were, she reminded them sadly. What kind of a life was that going to be for heaven's sakes?

"Angie's going to have her hair cut," Angie's mother interrupted to change the subject. "I think it's a fine idea. I've thought for a long time that her hair might be causing all those headaches."

Angie smiled faintly, not wanting to agree or disagree. The headaches wouldn't bother her again, not for years and years, and she wouldn't have to take the tranquilizers either.

She went into her bedroom and gazed at herself in the mirror, holding her palms against her hair at the side of her face, trying to see what she'd look like. In a way she felt strange not to be able to guess what the years immediately ahead would be like. Years without Grandmother and without Jeff. Sadness touched her and then abruptly was gone.

There were no immediate plans. In a few days or maybe a few weeks they would hear from the men at the university. Taking part in the experiments might be fun. She would seem like another person.

I am fifteen, she told herself solemnly. In a little while I'll be sixteen. By the time I'm a grown woman, people will have forgotten that I was ever Angie. She had the most peculiar sensation that she had been carrying a heavy load for a very long time, but now she was free of it.

And ahead of her was the unknown promise of tomorrow.